MURDER ᴍOST REMOTE

WATERFELL TWEED COZY MYSTERY SERIES:
BOOK FOUR

MONA MARPLE

For the writers who encouraged me to be a reader
And the readers who encourage me to be a writer

*T*he fire was intense, a ball of angry heat attacking her face as she climbed up the melting staircase to rescue more books.

"Help!" She called, but her voice was lost in the flames.

Another step gave way under her weight, causing her to hang from the wooden rail as the fire ebbed closer.

Sandy woke with a jump, her heart pounding in her chest as her eyes acclimatised to the cool dark of her bedroom. She choked back tears and forced herself to feel the welcome cold air on her body. She had tossed the sheets from the bed and only had her thin pyjamas to protect her from either the heat or the chill, depending on whether she was asleep or awake.

As her heartbeat returned to normal, Sandy picked her phone up from the bedside table. Almost 5am. She stifled a yawn and climbed out of bed, her feet slipping straight into the expensive sheepskin slippers that Coral had bought for her last birthday. The soft curls of the wool enveloped her toes and pushed the nightmare further from the forefront of her mind.

Her small suitcase sat empty by the bedroom door and from within it, two piercing green eyes watched her.

"Oh cat!" She cursed as she rose to her feet. "I've told you not up here! Go on, get downstairs."

The green eyes continued to stare at her and she sighed in resignation. The still unnamed cat had quickly asserted itself to be in charge in her home.

Sandy ignored the queasy feeling in her stomach, the aftermath of the nightmare, and dragged her weary body into a hot shower, where she forced herself to read the instructions on the back of the shampoo bottle to keep her thoughts in check.

She spent longer than usual styling her hair in a bid to ignore the suitcase, and at exactly the time he had said, she heard Tom's car pull up outside. She caught herself giving a wide grin towards the cat, who watched her with disdain from his new sitting place, her pillow.

"A smile wouldn't hurt you, you know." She muttered. The cat was so dark and fluffy it was impossible to pick out his nose or mouth. Only his piercing eyes broke up the pure black of his coat. He was beautiful, Sandy had begun to tell people with pride.

As she left the house, she glanced up at her bedroom window, but the cat wasn't there. She shook her head at her idea that he may have been there to see her off to work.

"What's got into you?" Tom asked with a smile. He had reached over from the driver seat to open the passenger door for her.

"I left the cat curled up in my bed. On my pillow even! I'm getting far too soft in my old age." Sandy explained as she climbed into the car. "Thanks for picking me up."

Tom shrugged, his attention on the rear view mirror as

he indicated to move off from the pavement. "You look beautiful. I like your hair like that."

"I had some extra time. I've been up hours." Sandy explained.

"Packing finally?" He asked.

Sandy felt her cheeks flush. "Erm, no."

Tom glanced across at her as he waited for a red light to change. "The dream again?"

She bit her lip as she nodded.

"It's going to be okay, you know?" Tom said. "I'm in the same boat, but we've both got good people who can manage fine without us in their way."

"I know." Sandy said. "I just wonder if it's a good idea."

"A whole shop's stock for a bargain price, Sand, of course it's a good idea." Tom reminded her. She couldn't argue with that. Books and Bakes was in desperate need of fresh book stock, and this was a rare opportunity to get a whole shop's stock for an unbelievably low price.

"I just have this feeling, this gut feeling..." Sandy began.

"Vibes?" Tom asked with a smile.

"No, I'll leave the vibes to Dorie." Sandy said with a laugh. "You're right. I'm being silly, everything will be fine."

Tom nodded as he pulled up outside Books and Bakes. "Our first weekend away. It's going to be better than fine."

Sandy allowed herself to relax and gave him a genuine smile as he planted a delicate kiss on her lips.

"I'll pick you up at 2, okay?"

"Okay." She agreed as she climbed out of the car.

Books and Bakes was already open. She was showing her face only because she had insisted to Tom that she wanted to do one last check that everything was in order. He had wanted to set off first thing in the morning, and she knew that made more sense given the long drive they had ahead of them, but when he had realised how anxious she was about the time away, he had agreed that they each spend the morning on last jobs in their businesses before setting off.

Tom had been packed for days and texted her several times each day with a countdown, in hours, of how long until they would set off. Sandy had ignored the suitcase since borrowing it from her sister, Coral.

But she could put it off no longer.

"Good morning, Sandy." Dorie Slaughter called out as Sandy pushed open the door. Dorie, the cafe's most loyal customer, was sitting alone as usual.

"Just the woman, Dorie. Can I pick your brains?" Sandy asked.

Dorie let out a tremendous sigh. "I guess I have a minute if you're quick."

"I can ask someone else if you're too busy." Sandy said.

"No, no, you'll get the best information from me, don't waste your time with anyone else. I can spare a minute."

Sandy smiled to herself. "What do you do when your gut is telling you something's a bad idea?"

The question surprised Dorie so much she almost choked on her tea. "That's your question? You've interrupted my precious little quiet time to ask me that?"

"Well, I..." Sandy began.

"You listen to it, of course!" Dorie exclaimed with an eye roll.

"It's that simple?" Sandy asked.

"Lord help me." Dorie said, although her interest in religion seemed only to extend as far as church events that involved food, or the potential for gossip. "Yes, it's that simple Sandy. Never, ever, ignore your gut."

Sandy gulped. "Ok. I guess that's pretty clear then."

"What are you doing here?" Coral called from the counter, where she held a single cake stand, free from a cake on top. Her ability to carry more than a single object at a time hadn't improved since she had joined Books and Bakes.

"Nice to see you too." Sandy quipped. "I wanted to check everything's okay."

"We've told you all week, everything's fine." Coral replied. "Just go and enjoy yourself, sis."

"Fridays can be busy, maybe I can serve for a bit?" Sandy offered. Derrick had agreed, with some reluctance, to return to the bookshop counter upstairs. While he preferred to be on his feet and active, he seemed incapable of refusing a request made by Sandy.

"Sandy, we're fine, get out of here!" Bernice scolded, emerging from the kitchen with a balance of cakes and brownies in her arms. "We all want to keep our jobs, and to do that, we need you up in Scotland buying new stock."

Sandy grimaced at the reminder of how uncertain jobs had been before she had extended the bookshop to occupy the upper floor.

"Scotland, eh?" Dorie asked. "Lovely place. Never been, but I saw an antiques show up there once. Ooh, beautiful it was."

"It's not a holiday." Sandy blurted. "I'm looking at new stock."

"Driving all that way to look at books?" Dorie asked, her nose wrinkled with disapproval. As loyal as she was to the cafe part of Sandy's business, she had no interest in literature. "Can't you use your magic phones and thingy-ma-jigs to do that?"

"Sometimes." Sandy admitted. "They're all in storage this time, though. I need to go up there and have a good look at them."

"Hmm." Dorie grunted, her interest in the bookish conversation exhausted. "Think you'll find any new recipes up there?"

Bernice cleared her throat.

"Not that the same old recipes every day aren't nice." Dorie said, shooting a syrupy sweet smile towards Bernice.

"I'll make sure I try out a Scottish cafe or two, in your honour." Sandy agreed. She squeezed past Coral and stood behind the counter. Everything was tidy and in place. The cafe was almost full and several customers had books on their tables that they had either already paid for or would buy after they'd finished their food and drink.

Things certainly looked in order.

"It's like watching a new mum leave their baby." Bernice said with a shake of her head as she returned to the kitchen. Sandy followed her, although the spot check was unnecessary. Bernice brought a military attention to all she did, and her baking and managing of the Books and Bakes kitchen was no exception.

"Are you sure you're happy that I'm going?" Sandy asked as Bernice busied herself wiping down the counters.

"What's going on, Sandy?" Bernice asked. She turned to look at her employer, kitchen spray in one hand and a cloth in the other. "You've left us before without all of this. Are you nervous about going away with Tom?"

Sandy shook her head. Although it would be the longest period of time spent with Tom, and their first time away from Waterfell Tweed together, Sandy was looking forward to that part of the trip. Their lives in the village were so busy, and so full of other people's demands, both for her running Books and Bakes and for Tom as landlord of The Tweed public house, the idea of a weekend away as a couple made her feel warm and content inside.

"Well, what is it? You can tell me, whatever it is." Bernice coaxed.

"I just have this feeling like I shouldn't go." Sandy said, with a shrug. "I can't explain it."

Bernice gazed at her, her auburn hair pinned on top of her head and dusted with flour as always. She narrowed her eyes and the intensity of her stare made Sandy look away.

"Well." Bernice said after a few awkward seconds had passed. "The shop needs stock, and if you don't want to get it, I guess I'll have to."

"What?" Sandy asked, as Bernice placed the cloth and cleaning product on the counter and washed her hands.

"I'll go." Bernice said. "Have you got the address?"

"No!" Sandy exclaimed. The strength of her reaction surprised them both. Sandy couldn't explain what she was feeling, but she knew that if someone had to make this trip, it had to be her. "No, no. I'm being silly. Sorry, Bernice, I don't what's come over me."

Bernice raised her eyebrows and smiled. "Love. That's what's come over you."

Sandy allowed herself a small smile as her cheeks flushed crimson.

She said her goodbyes and left the shop. She would walk home, the fresh air would do her good. Coral had borrowed her car while hers was being repaired after a minor collision with a dry stone wall.

She allowed the walk to clear her head, resisting the urge to put her headphones in and listen to music or a mystery audio book. She had little silence in her life and felt a need for some.

When she returned home, she had just a few short hours to check which of her clothes were clean and pack for her weekend away. The cat was fast asleep in her bed, and

Sandy noticed how he let out tiny, contented purrs as she worked quietly around him, collecting fleece jackets and walking boots, t-shirts and jeans. It was a practical wardrobe, designed to help convince her that she was indeed a practical woman.

By the time Tom pulled up outside her cottage, her reaction was as much nerves as excitement.

Because as much as she tried, she couldn't shake the ominous feeling that she shouldn't be going on the trip.

That something bad lay in store.

2
___

"Have you been to Scotland before?" Sandy asked. They had been driving for four hours before they had stopped for dinner at a motorway service station. Sandy had tried not to show her disappointment at eating pre-packed sandwiches while Tom appeared to be just pleased for a break from the road.

He shook his head, his mouth full of the chicken curry he had chosen from the hot food selection. A stale-looking naan bread sat untouched on his tray. He was ravenous, shoveling the curry and rice in his mouth from overflowing forkfuls without conversation. He looked at her then and gave a self-conscious smile. "Sorry, I'm starving."

"It's ok. I'm sorry you're doing all the driving." She apologised.

"Don't be, I'm happy to be here as your chauffeur."

"You're more than my chauffeur." Sandy said, and she reached across the table and took his hand in hers. The gesture made him blush a little.

"Even better." He said with a grin, then noticed her uneaten sandwich. "Don't you like it? Curry's good."

"I'm a bit of a sandwich snob." Sandy admitted. "One of the problems of working in the food business, I can spot cheap ingredients like a... sorry, I don't want to put you off."

"I'd eat a dead horse to be honest, you won't put me off." Tom said. He tore the naan bread in half and used one half to mop up the remaining curry sauce, then bit a chunk of it and began to chew.

Sandy sat back and took in the scene around them. Dozens of couples seeking a break from whatever journeys they were on were sat at tables drinking coffee and scrolling on smart phones. A group of workmen in hi-vis vests erupted into a burst of laughter from the fast food queue. A young mum with pristine make-up and a slender figure watched with glee as her baby walked across the seating area towards her, their tiny hands in the much bigger ones of a balding father.

The mundanity of the scene felt intimate somehow. To be sat with a man she liked, taking a break from a long drive. It was so normal, so routine, and yet an experience she hadn't shared in a long time.

"You ok?" Tom asked. His plate was empty and he had just peeled a banana.

She nodded, unsure how to explain the way she felt.

"Let's get back out there." Tom said. He practically inhaled the banana and placed the peel on his plate, then pushed his chair back and stood up.

As they walked back into the cold afternoon air of the car park, Tom took her hand in his and gave it a squeeze.

**

When they finally reached the Isle of Mull, Tom could barely keep his eyes open.

"Let's go and get a nap." Sandy said as he stifled another enormous yawn.

"No, I'll be fine." He said.

"Tom. You're exhausted. I'm not taking no for an answer on this." She insisted. Tom glanced at her, his eyes small and red, and nodded his agreement.

Sandy had booked a small bed and breakfast for them at a bargain price, and couldn't believe that her last minute booking had been possible at all. She had never seen a place as beautiful as Mull, with its dramatic landscape and quiet isolation.

When they had checked in and been shown to their rooms, Tom disappeared into his room and Sandy sat by the window in her own. The view was out to the bay, where the sand was white enough to be Caribbean but the waves roared and crashed with force. Sandy pulled her opal cardigan further around her body without realising and allowed the time to pass watching the waves build and trying to guess which would make the biggest crash against the sand.

The knock on her door some time later made her jump. The sky was growing a deep blue as night approached. She gave in to a yawn as she padded across the small room and opened the door.

"Ready?" Tom asked. The sight of him made her grin. His face looked well-rested but his hair was stood at all angles, it's usual neat appearance changed by the tossing and turning of his nap. "I've been texting you."

"Sorry!" Sandy said, gesturing to the inside of her room. "I sat in the windowsill to look at the view and never moved away. It's so beautiful here."

Tom blushed. "My eyes were closed before I made it to the bed, so I'll have to take your word for it."

"Are you sure you don't want to put this off to the morning?" Sandy asked. She had arranged a late meeting time with the retired bookseller, who had been slow to agree to anything after normal business hours despite their long journey. Sandy had wondered how desperate he really was to sell the stock and was feeling apprehensive about the viewing. She couldn't stand the thought that she may have subjected Tom to such a long drive for a wasted journey.

"Nah, let's get it done and then tomorrow's ours." Tom said. Sandy nodded. They had a full day to enjoy the island before heading back to Waterfell Tweed.

The winds hit Sandy as soon as she pushed the bed and breakfast front door open. She ran across the road to where Tom's car was parked and opened the door to let herself in.

"Anyone would think you'd never felt a gust of wind before." Tom teased as he joined her several seconds later after a relaxed stroll across to the car.

"I don't mind it back home, but I thought you were supposed to get better weather on holiday!" Sandy said with a laugh as Tom entered the postcode for the storage unit and began to drive.

"Good point." Tom said.

They drove in a comfortable silence down tiny, winding roads with fields on either sides. Occasionally a sheep stood in the middle of the road and refused to let them pass. Every new scene seemed to be more beautiful and breathtaking than the last.

"Seriously?" Tom asked in disbelief as he slammed the brakes on the car. Sandy forced her gaze, which had been looking out of her window to the sea, back to the road ahead of them, where a group of enormous Highland cattle stood. They had blocked the road entirely.

"Oh, wow. They're beautiful." Sandy said. The creatures were taller than the car and covered in a thick, shaggy caramel coat. Giant horns protruded from their heads. Sandy moved to open the car door.

"Stop!" Tom called. He dove across the car to take her hand from the door handle, then gave an awkward cough and moved back across to the driver's side.

"What was that about?" Sandy asked in amusement. Tom's cheeks were red, his forehead looked moist.

"I, erm, well, they're dangerous animals…" Tom stuttered.

"Are you scared of cows, Tom Nelson?" Sandy asked with a raised eyebrow.

"Not scared, Sandy Shaw, just sensibly cautious. They're bigger than me, those animals, so they're definitely bigger than you!"

"What are we going to do, then? We need to get these wild beasts off the road. This guy's already annoyed enough to have to see us this late. We can't keep him waiting." Sandy said.

Tom shrugged his broad shoulders then pressed the horn.

The cows moved across to the field and, luckily, not towards the car. Their movements were leisurely, as if they were used to being sounded out of the road, which they probably were. One of the largest defiantly left its front legs on the road and, as Tom drove slowly past the group, the cow's face was just inches from his window.

"We survived!" Sandy said with a laugh. "They are stunning, aren't they? What a sight. I wish we weren't in such a rush, I'd have sat there happily and just watched them."

Tom gave her a strange look. "You have an unnatural interest in Highland cows, Sandy."

Sandy laughed. It was true, actually. She liked all animals. One of her favourite games as a child had been pretending to be a cat or a dog. She would crawl around the house while her mum dusted and polished, meowing or woofing, until her mum would fetch her a bowl of water and set it down on the kitchen floor. The memory made her smile and think of how the cat had entered her life. She'd almost forgotten how much she liked animals, it had been so long since she'd had a pet. She really must give the cat a name.

"Here we are." Tom said. He had turned onto what could barely be called a track. Fisherman's Bluff, said a tattered sign nailed to a tree.

Sandy glanced at Tom but he was focused on the path.

The track gradually climbed a hill, winding around groups of trees, until they reached the highest point, where the cliff edge was revealed to them. The sea, now reflecting the dark blue sky with moonlight shimmers bouncing from the waves, was just metres away.

Sandy felt her stomach contract. "Are you sure this is the right place? I can't believe a storage unit's up here?"

As she said the words, a light flashed ahead of them. Headlights. Tom continued to drive towards them and as they drew closer, a large barn was revealed in the darkness. An old Land Rover, not dissimilar to Sandy's trusty vehicle back home, was parked outside and a man stepped out as Tom parked a few metres ahead of him.

"Sandy Shaw?" The man asked in an accent she couldn't place.

She nodded and held out her hand, which he shook once with a firm grip.

"Tom Nelson." Tom said and he offered his own hand. The man gave him such a firm handshake that Sandy heard Tom's hand crack.

"Books are in 'ere." The man said. He turned and lead Sandy and Tom towards the barn, which was even bigger up close. He pressed a button on a keypad and the metal doors opened wide, revealing a modern and brightly-lit interior that was bursting with cardboard boxes.

"Wow." Sandy said.

"Ignore the smell." The man said, but offered no further explanation. Sandy guessed that the barn usually housed animals and wondered where they had been sent to make room for the books. "Go on, take a look."

Sandy stepped forward into the barn, overwhelmed by the sheer amount of boxes there were.

"They won't bite." The man said, with a laugh. He opened one of the boxes and Sandy peered in. Military history books. She began to examine a few titles as the man opened other boxes for her. Every book she checked was in immaculate condition.

"Are they all in this condition?" She asked.

The man looked at her with his mouth set tight. "I'm not tryin' to con ya, lass. You need books, I need rid. That's it."

Sandy's cheeks flushed. "I didn't mean to..."

"I know." The man said. He was abrupt and Sandy realised that this wasn't easy for him. That saying farewell to his book shop had been a hard decision to make.

She nodded and returned her attention to the boxes he had opened, feeling obligated to at least glance at them all. They were all full of specialist interest titles, the things that readers would travel for, and pay a fair price for.

"What price are you looking for?" Sandy asked.

He named a price that was even lower than she had been lead to expect.

"I'll take them all." She said. "I can organise for them to be collected in the next few days, if that's okay?"

The man nodded and held out his hand. Sandy braced herself and allowed him to shake her hand again.

"Pleasure doin' business with ye." The man said. He lead them out of the barn, the shutter closing as he did, and for a moment Sandy thought she had become blind. The world had become perfectly black in the time she had been in the barn. She placed her hand in front of her face and was stunned to note that she couldn't see it at all.

She reached out for Tom's hand and felt him jump.

"Steady on lass, your husband'll be after me guts." The man exclaimed, and Sandy realised she had grabbed the wrong man.

"Oh my! I'm so sorry! It's so dark out here, sorry, I..."

Tom clicked his car keys and the headlights illuminated the short distance to the car. Sandy grabbed hold of Tom and walked carefully with him back to the vehicle. By the time they climbed in the car, the other man had already started his engine and moved to drive past them. He gave a wave as he went.

"Oh my gosh, Tom." Sandy gushed as she put on her seatbelt.

"Worth the trip?"

"It's an absolute bargain!" She said. "This new stock is a huge opportunity. It could really get me known as a quality bookshop for specialist interest books. I could squeal."

"Please don't." Tom scolded. "I don't want you attracting those Highland cattle again."

Sandy laughed and reached across the car to give Tom's hand a squeeze.

"Thank you for doing this for me." She said.

"It's my pleasure, Sand. I mean, we're right by the cliffs in the darkest place that I've ever been to on Earth. What could possibly go wrong?"

3

Sandy watched as Tom devoured his black pudding. She cupped the mug of mocha that the bed and breakfast owner had agreed to make her when Sandy produced a sachet from her handbag, and gazed out of the window across the fields. The scenery was even more entrancing in full daylight, and the sun was out and bright in the sky.

Finally, her own breakfast arrived.

Sandy waited for the woman to return to the kitchen, then whispered to Tom. "It's like she's related to Coral, bringing one plate out at a time."

Tom nodded, his mouth full of sausage and egg. "If she's related to Coral, she's related to you."

"Hmm, good point." Sandy said. She had opted for beans on toast, not wanting a large, heavy breakfast, but she was envious as she watched Tom work his way through his full Scottish.

"Want some?" He asked as if he had read her thoughts.

She grinned and reached across the table with her fork,

then speared the end of his sausage and took a bite. "Mmm."

"So, what shall we do today?" Tom asked as she chewed. The meat was delicious and she could tell it was high-quality. She regretted her beans on toast even more. "I saw this in the hallway for guided tours of Mull Castle, do you fancy that?"

He pushed a leaflet across the small table towards her and Sandy picked it up. The cover featured a photograph of an old castle, complete with Scottish flag flying proudly. She looked at the inside of the leaflet and saw how stunning the architecture of the castle appeared in several photographs.

"Mull Castle, eh? Seen better days that place has." The B&B woman said. She had appeared at the table with a plate piled high with doorstep-thick white toast smothered in butter.

"Isn't that the point with a castle?" Tom quipped.

The woman raised an eyebrow in response, then shuffled away, her pink slippers worn down on the sides.

Sandy giggled as she retreated into the kitchen. "That was cheeky, Tom."

"I don't think the Scottish get my sense of humour." Tom said. "There was a Scottish boy in my class at school and he never liked me."

"Ooh, such extensive research!" Sandy laughed.

Tom grinned, revealing the dimple in his cheek. He was so handsome and at ease with her. "So, fancy the run down castle?"

Sandy nodded. "I do, actually. I've not been stomping around a castle since I was little."

She could vaguely remember a trip out to a historic fortress with Coral and her mum as a child. She didn't know where her father had been, but in her memory he was absent. She remembered the building being almost rubble, and imagined that it must have been closed for years now as the world became more aware of health and safety. But back then, with the sun on her freckled face, she had hung from a window hole high in the air, the only thing preventing her fall being a flimsy length of rope.

"Let's get going then." Tom said. He mopped up his baked bean juice with a slice of toast and took a bite, and Sandy took a long, last sip of her mocha. Although it was sunny outside, she knew it would be cold, and was glad she'd got several layers of clothing on. She quickly thought of how many couples spent their first holidays in sun-drenched destinations where they could show off toned bodies and flattering summer clothes, and shook her head in amusement. Her vest top, jumper, scarf and rain mac made her look shapeless, but she didn't mind. She was finally growing confident in her own skin.

Tom stood up and pulled his own rain mac on, as the B&B woman appeared by their table again. They seemed to be the only guests she had.

"Off out then?" She asked as she gazed up at Tom with a girlish grin on her ruddy face.

"We're going to brave Mull Castle." Tom said as he double-wrapped his scarf around his neck.

The woman shook her head, causing her fleshy cheeks to wobble. "You tourists can't find enough ways to waste your money."

"Thank you for breakfast." Sandy said to try and change the subject.

"You've not finished yours." The woman said, and Sandy looked at her plate. The toast had grown cold and soggy underneath the beans while she had been busy looking at Tom's full Scottish. "See what I mean? Wasting money."

Sandy felt her cheeks flush. "I'm sorry, it was very nice, I'm just not very hungry."

"Sandy has her own cafe." Tom offered by way of explanation as Sandy silently urged him to stop talking. "She finds it hard to eat in other establishments."

The woman glanced between the two, her eyes beady and intense. "I'll remember that tomorrow."

"Come on, Tom, we need to go." Sandy urged. Tom gave her an awkward smile and followed her out of the dining room and down the hallway, then through the front door and out into the fresh air.

He unlocked the car door and climbed into the driver's seat, then punched a postcode into the sat nav.

"She seems nice." He said after a few moments as he began to drive. Sandy's head jerked towards him and she checked his face for any sign he was being ironic. "It must be strange living out here, don't you think?"

Sandy considered the question. As beautiful as the Isle of Mull was, it was barren. They had seen only a few buildings on the island so far, and hadn't passed another vehicle on their journey. There were small clusters of shops and pubs, but Sandy doubted they would have time to explore those.

"I'd love a few days here." She admitted.

"Really? I thought you were chomping at the bit to get back?" Tom asked.

"Yeah." Sandy said carefully. She had been nervous about leaving Books and Bakes, but now that she was away from Waterfell Tweed, with Tom all to herself, the thought of just a few more days away to relax seemed like bliss. "I guess I've realised they can cope without me. And I'd like to see that little..."

"Tobermory?" Tom prompted.

"That's it!" Sandy exclaimed. "You've heard about it?"

He nodded. "It looks beautiful. I could spend a few hours in the pub there watching the world go by. Wow, talk about a busman's holiday - take the publican to the pub!"

Sandy laughed. "I wouldn't mind keeping you company in a cosy pub."

Her phone beeped then and she glanced down to see a new message. She could feel the heat of Tom watching her as he pulled over to allow a car to pass on the single-lane road.

"Bernice." Sandy said as she swiped to unlock the phone.

"What does it say?" Tom asked.

"Stop worrying! Everything's fine here. Glad the books were what we need - see you tomorrow."

"Tomorrow?" Tom exclaimed. "We won't be home before the cafe closes."

"I'm sure it's just a mistake." Sandy said nervously. "I'm sure she isn't expecting me back in work tomorrow."

Tom nodded, but the mood in the car changed as they approached the castle. Her relaxed, holiday vibe had disappeared. She suddenly felt guilty for being away from the shop, as if she had rang in sick when all she wanted to do was have a day at home watching a trash TV marathon.

"You're doing it." Tom said.

She looked at him and realised that she was on the edge of tears.

"Oh, Sandy. Bernice is more than capable of running the shop. Not saying you're not needed or anything, but you've been out a fair bit investigating the murders lately. They've all learnt how to manage without you."

"That's true." Sandy said. "How do you manage to take time away from The Tweed without feeling guilty?"

Tom flashed a smile. "I don't take any time away. So I'm probably not the best person to give advice. What are we like, eh?"

Sandy smiled and stroked the top of his arm gently.

She'd heard the natural way he described them as 'we' and enjoyed the warm sensation it gave her.

4

*M*ull Castle sat atop a bluff, visible for the last ten minutes of their slow journey on the narrow, winding roads.

"Wow." Sandy said as she walked up the grassy hill, her hand linked with Tom's.

"Impressive, isn't it? I'd have loved this place as a boy!"

It was easy to see why. The castle itself was everything a child would love and even Sandy expected a dragon to fly out from behind it at any moment.

"Hurry up!" A shrill voice shouted down at them from the top of the hill. A small man with large glasses and a gleaming bald head stood in front of the castle, waving his arms madly towards them. "Hurry up!"

Sandy and Tom glanced at each other, shrugged, and increased the pace of their walk until they were level with the man.

"Is everything okay?" Sandy asked, her words laboured with shortness of breath.

"You're late!" The man exclaimed with a glance at his

watch. "It's really not okay to keep others waiting. Let's move it."

He set off at a brisk pace towards the castle and Sandy followed him.

"What are we late for?" Tom asked.

The man turned, his face red with exasperation. "The guided tour, of course! You're the last two. Hurry along! I really can't make it any clearer."

"Come on, Tom." Sandy called, with a wink. He walked quickly and caught up with her.

"We're not booked on the tour." He whispered to her.

She flashed him a mischievous smile. "I think it'll be fun. And whoever he thinks we are, they're clearly not coming."

A cunning smile crept across Tom's face. "I like this side of you, Sandy Shaw."

**

The tour guide led Sandy and Tom through an archway that took them to the gardens within the castle grounds. Sandy imagined that the space may have once been a trading ground, or market area, but it now served as a picnic space. A group of tourists sat on picnic benches in stony silence.

"The latecomers are here." The guide said. He threw his hands up in the air.

"What kept y'all?" An elderly woman in a fur coat asked in an American twang.

"We had trouble finding the place." Tom said. "Our apologies."

"Is that all of us now?" A teenage girl with a pixie haircut asked in the same accent as the older woman.

"Yes, this is it." The guide said. "If I can have your attention, please. The tour will last for roughly one hour. It is a walking tour and we must remain together. The castle is in most ways exactly as it was back when it was built, so expect small spaces and dark areas. If you are squeamish or unfit, you should consider staying here. At the end of the tour, I will answer questions. Let's go."

"Erm, excuse me, sir?" A man with wild curly hair called.

"They're all American." Sandy whispered to Tom, who looked at her and nodded.

"Questions at the end!" The guide called.

"You haven't told us your name, sir." The curly-haired man said.

The guide turned back to them with a grin. "Ah, how silly of me. I'm Graeme O'Connell, tour guide extraordinaire."

"Ooh!" The older woman said. She met Sandy's gaze and flashed a smile, revealing a spot of red lipstick on her front tooth. "Don't y'all worry about being late, now, we won't hold it against you."

"Mother." A man in a floral shirt said under his breath.

"Here we go, I'm in trouble again." The woman said. She rolled her eyes in Sandy's direction and Sandy grinned at her.

The American group appeared to be headed by the older woman, the matriarch. Her three sons were all different - the floral-shirt man appeared artistic, the second had the curly hair, and the third was as bald as Graeme O'Connell. But their bone structure made it obvious they were brothers. Two appeared to have wives, and there were two teenagers, the pixie-haired girl and a boy who looked so All-American he could have just walked in from baseball practice.

Sandy and Tom walked behind them, trying not to listen to the hushed conversations they were trying to hide from the tour guide.

Graeme lead them into the castle through a grand wooden door.

"Would ya look at this, isn't it swell?" The floral-shirt man exclaimed as he placed his hand over his mouth. He turned to look at Sandy then and his cheeks grew pink. "Where are my manners? I'm Teddy, pleased to meet y'all."

"Oh!" Sandy said in surprise. It hadn't occurred to her to exchange pleasantries with the other group members. "I'm Sandy, and this is Tom."

Tom smiled at Teddy. "You don't get things like this over in the States, huh?"

"The oldest thing in my city is probably a Starbucks!" Teddy said and roared with laughter. A woman with plumped-up lips and eyebrows that sat unnaturally high on her face gave an unreadable expression towards him. "And oh, my lovely wife, Priscilla."

Sandy smiled in the woman's direction, then turned her attention to the grand passageway they had entered. The interior was grey stone, with a row of arches along one side, and a grand staircase up ahead. It was breathtaking.

"Mull Castle dates back to 1927." Graeme O'Connell explained. "It was…"

"1927?" Tom queried. "I've got living relatives older than that."

"Ah, just testing." Graeme gushed. "Glad you're paying attention. Mull Castle dates back to 1727. It was first home to Lady Margaret of Mull. The staircase, as you'll see, dominates this area and was intended to allow Lady Margaret to make a grand entrance."

"Sounds like you, Priscilla." The older woman heading the family called.

Priscilla attempted to frown but her forehead refused to crease.

"Mother, really." The man with curly hair muttered. He was standing next to the teenage boy, who appeared to be trying hard to keep his eyes open.

"Eli, how refreshing for a man to defend a lady's honour." Priscilla spat as she glared at her husband. Teddy avoided her gaze and flashed a sweet smile at his mother instead.

"We'll move on." Graeme said. He seemed to be unaware of the trouble in his camp. He led them past the stone arches into a long, empty room. A small window stood at the far end and the room was lit by fires along the length of the space.

"What was this room for?" Tom asked. Sandy gave his hand a squeeze, touched by his curiosity.

Graeme spun on his heels and made dramatic eye contact with Tom. "This is the space where Lady Margaret's spirit returns to chase tour parties like ours out of her castle."

"Hmm." Tom said. "I more meant what was it used for when she was alive?"

Graeme sighed. "We don't know."

Sandy stifled a giggle.

"Sir, do you think we'll see a ghost today?" Teddy in his floral shirt asked.

"There's every chance we will, yes." Graeme replied.

"And what's the procedure if we do?" The older woman asked.

"Marlene, please." The other woman, whose hair was in a pixie cut like the teenage girl's, and whose attention had been on her smart phone up to then, said through gritted teeth. "Don't scare the children."

The teenage boy rolled his eyes at the suggestion he was a child.

"Devon, we need to be prepared." Marlene replied. "So, Graeme, what should we do if we hear any bumps or shrieks or whatever?"

"Well." Graeme said. He was at the point furthest away from the various fires and his expression was hard to read. "We're the only people in the castle today. So if you hear anything at all, my advice would be to stay together. Or run. Whichever you prefer."

"Stay together or run. Do you hear that everyone? You two at the back, did you hear that?" Marlene called.

"Yes, thank you. Stay together or run, got it." Tom replied. He flashed an easy smile in Marlene's direction.

"Do you think this could have been a room for eating?" Teddy asked.

"No, we'll come to the banquet hall shortly." Graeme said. He continued to stand still, and Tom and Sandy walked away from the group slightly to explore the room. The stonework was immaculate, the details of the shape along the walls so intricate it would challenge a modern day stonemason.

"Are you enjoying this?" Sandy asked.

"God yeah." Tom admitted. "It's like being five years old again and playing dungeons and dragons. Can you imagine the things that have happened in here?"

"Well, not with the tour guide we've got, no." Sandy said with a laugh.

"He's clueless, isn't he? 1927!"

"Are you asking him questions just to see him panic and make things up?" Sandy asked.

A glint appeared in Tom's eyes. "I hadn't been, no, but that's a good idea."

They returned to the group, who hadn't moved. Teddy stood arm in arm with Marlene while his wife Priscilla stood with her arms crossed a few feet away.

"And on we must continue, we have many rooms to visit." Graeme said. He led the party through the rest of the long space and into a bedroom, complete with a four-poster bed draped in heavy material. A wooden chaise longue sat at the far end of the room, next to a roaring open fireplace. A portrait of a young woman with sad eyes, dressed in furs, hung from the wall over the fireplace.

"Ooh, is that her? The Princess?" Teddy asked.

"Lady Margaret of Mull." Graeme corrected. "There's never been a princess here."

"Oh. It says Princess Murdina in the corner." Teddy said.

Graeme proffered a false smile towards Teddy. "It was incredibly dangerous for a woman to live alone back then. A Princess is assumed to have a Prince, or a King, to protect her. Lady Margaret used many aliases to ensure her safety."

"That one almost sounds believable," Tom whispered in Sandy's ear.

"Erm, Graeme," Sandy called. "are you Scottish?"

The man appeared stunned by her question. "Of course I'm not. Do I sound Scottish?"

"No, you don't actually... I just wondered. With all your knowledge. I wondered if you might be a distant relative, perhaps."

"I can assure you there's no Scottish in me at all." Graeme mumbled. "Now, if we can stay focused on the tour. This is of course the master bedroom. Although it was a mistress who slept here. This is almost identical to how it would have looked when Lady Margaret herself was in residence."

"It's so fancy!" Marlene gushed. "What do you think Trixie?"

The teenage girl wrinkled her nose. "Dark."

"Well of course, there's no electricity!"

"There is electricity in some parts of the castle." Graeme said. "We keep these smaller rooms lit by fire as they would have been originally, but the current owner of the castle modernised it considerably. There's running water, electricity, even WiFi and a toilet."

"Who is the owner now?" The curly-haired man, Eli, asked.

"We're not allowed to disclose his name. He's a very wealthy businessman. He bought the castle to restore it."

"Impressive." Eli said.

"Always the business man, dad." The teenage boy said with an eye roll.

Eli shrugged his shoulders. "Someone has to look after the numbers."

"You know mom opened a savings account for me." The teenage son said.

Eli gave a tight smile. "That's great champ. You'll have to give me the details so I can put some money in there for you too."

The boy grinned. "Really? That's great dad, I mean I don't have the details but mom could give them to you. You could ask her."

Eli nodded his head once but made no further comment. The boy's smile retreated.

"Would Lady Margaret have kept the fire on all day and night?" Priscilla asked.

"Oh yes. It wasn't just the lighting, remember, it was the heat source."

"But she had slaves to do that?"

"Servants, yes. We expect she would have had at least 10 servants. There are enough bedrooms for them all to have lived here."

"She'd have let her slaves live with her?" Priscilla asked.

"For goodness sake, Priscilla, stop saying slaves." Marlene barked at her. "You're giving Americans a bad name."

Sandy glanced at Tom, who was trying to keep a straight face.

"We're not all like that, I promise." Marlene called through the small crowd to Sandy and Tom. "In our history, you probably don't know about US history, but we have an awful history with slaves. Not us personally, of course, but the Deep South has some sins to be forgiven for."

"Amen." Trixie said. She had the look of a girl with a strong moral compass.

"Please, don't worry about us." Sandy explained. "We're enjoying a rare day away from work, somewhere nice and quiet."

"Quiet? Ha! And then you met us." Teddy said.

Sandy flinched as Marlene licked the tip of her finger, gazed at her son, and rubbed at his cheek.

5

"*A*nd here, is the grand banquet hall." Graeme said with a flourish. The space was cavernous and lit by modern chandeliers. Three fireplaces were empty and unlit. The hall was filled with a table big enough to seat at least 50 people, and a display case ran along the length of one wall, filled with various objects. "This really is the highlight of this tour, and we'll spend some time in here. Please, feel free to move around and look. Do not try to sit at the table and don't touch anything on the table or in the case."

"What are all these things?" Marlene asked as she looked at the display case.

"They're things gathered from the time period of Lady Margaret. Some of the items belonged to Lady Margaret herself, such as the hairbrush and trinket box. They're very valuable."

"Can we take pictures?" Teddy asked.

"No, I'm afraid not." Graeme said. "No pictures. But please enjoy having a look around, and do ask any questions."

"What did Lady Margaret eat?" Trixie asked.

"Deer." Graeme said.

"Deer?" Trixie repeated. "Like, Bambi, deer?"

"And hog. Wild hog was popular. Deer was a delicacy. If the hunters could catch it, it would be the centrepiece of a dinner party."

"Jeff, didn't you serve deer last Thanksgiving?" Marlene asked her third son, the bald man who had remained silent so far.

"I doubt it." He said.

"We definitely didn't serve deer, Marlene." Devon, with the pixie cut, said.

"I think you did. It was definitely deer."

"You told me it was tofurkey, mom." Trixie whined.

"It was tofurkey, Trix."

"What on Earth is tofurkey?" Marlene asked. "Did you know about this, Jeff?"

"I know nothing about tofurkey." He said.

"I can't believe you made me eat deer." Trixie muttered.

"Geeze, Jeff, you know damn well it was tofurkey. We just told your mom it was turkey."

"Deer." Marlene corrected.

"Nobody mentioned deer!" Devon exclaimed. She saw Sandy watching her and gave an embarrassed smile, then returned her attention to her smart phone. She punched in a number, placed the phone to her ear, then cursed under her breath. "No signal, great."

"You need to make a call?" Jeff asked.

"I have a conference call. I told you I couldn't be here."

"But we all appreciate you making the effort, doll." Marlene said. "You have to stop work sometimes."

"I do stop work, like all the time. But the lab's right on the brink of something big. I should be there."

"You'll be home tomorrow." Jeff placated. "And me and Trixie love having you with us, don't we Trix?"

Trixie nodded.

Devon smiled at her daughter and pulled her in for a hug, then lead her towards the display case, leaving Tom and Sandy alone in front of the large table.

"These Yanks are a hoot." Tom whispered.

"I don't know, I think it's nice." Sandy said. "All of the family interactions, I don't have that. It must be nice to have relatives to annoy you."

"You've got Coral?" Tom quipped.

"She doesn't annoy me, though, not really. When you don't have many relatives, you can't really risk being annoyed by the one you do have."

"I get that." Tom said. "But this family are crazy. The one with all the plastic surgery?"

"Priscilla."

"See! You know their names!" Tom laughed. "Priscilla, okay, she hates the mother-in-law!"

"Really?" Sandy asked.

"Botox Face's husband is more of a mummy's boy than a husband. The two of them are walking around arm in arm while she's off scowling - except she can't scowl - on her own. It's comedy gold. Makes me think my family are normal."

Sandy shook her head and rolled her eyes. "I thought you were here for the castle experience, not the gossip."

"I get distracted easily." Tom said, with a laugh.

And then, the room went black.

A female let out a shriek.

"Priscilla, calm down for God's sake." A man's voice chided. "The power's gone, that's all."

"Everyone stay calm." Graeme's English accent implored

from across the darkness. "There's a trip switch, I'll stumble my way through the castle to find it."

"What shall we do?" Marlene's Southern drawl had grown familiar to Sandy. "Should we follow you?"

"No, no." Graeme said. "You Americans sue people too quickly, I don't want any of you walking into a wall and coming after my great wealth. Which amounts to around £25, if I'm honest. Just stay here. Stand still, please. I can't have anything damaged. I should only be a few minutes."

Sandy felt a hand reach for hers in the darkness and hoped it was Tom's. She wasn't scared of the dark, but there was something eerie about being in such a cavernous room without even a single window to offer natural light. They really were in the pitch black.

"You ok?" Tom whispered. He had reached over and tried to find her ear. The height difference meant he had actually whispered into the air a few inches above her head, so disoriented was he by the dark.

"Just hoping that Lady Margaret's ghost doesn't choose now to visit." Sandy admitted.

"Do you believe in all that? Ghosts?" Tom asked. His voice was louder and the noise made Sandy jump.

"Ghosts are very real, trust me." A voice came. Sandy thought it was Priscilla. Her tone always seemed whiny. It was an unfortunate voice to have to live with.

The conversation was disturbed by a noise, a whack of something falling to the floor. Then silence.

"Be careful!" A male voice commanded. "We all need to stay still."

"Where is he? This is the worst tour ever." The sulking tones of the teenage girl came.

"Trix..." Devon's voice chided.

"Wooooooooooo!" Tom called out by Sandy's side. She elbowed him in the ribs.

"You can cut out the ghost noises, Tom Nelson." Sandy said. She gave out an awkward laugh, wishing that Graeme O'Connell would return with light.

"Nelson?" Priscilla asked. It was impossible to tell whether she was standing directly in front of them, or off to one side, or even behind. "Are y'all related to the Nelsons of Nova Scotia?"

"Erm..." Tom stumbled. "Not to my knowledge?"

"Shame." Priscilla said.

Sandy turned her head to the left at the sight of a small light in the distance. A chill ran through her spine. "Tom, can you see that?"

A circular light danced around in the distance, slowly growing in size as it grew closer. Sandy thought of the orbs that were often supposed to accompany the spirits when they visited, and felt her heart race. Despite losing her parents at such a young age, one of her biggest fears had always been that they might decide to visit her from whatever afterlife they had gone on to.

She was torn between missing them desperately and being scared of ghostly forms.

"Thank goodness." Tom said, then raised his voice. "Looks like Graeme's on his way back."

As the light continued to grow bigger, Sandy realised it was a torch, and took a deep breath. She realised that her hands had been shaking, and clutched Tom's hand tighter. He gave her hand a squeeze and rubbed the palm with his thumb.

"Ladies and gentlemen." Graeme called out. "It's only the banquet hall that's affected. I don't know what's happened, I can only apologise. I'll use my trusty torch to highlight some of my favourite pieces in here, and then we can move on to the last rooms."

The group made muffled noises of agreement and Graeme shone the torch past them onto the table itself.

"If you look closely, you'll see how intricate the cutlery is. Every knife, fork and spoon features a unicorn head and dates back to the 1600s."

"Why a unicorn?" Tom asked.

"It's been a Scottish symbol since the 12th century." Graeme said. "Remember that Lady Margaret would have entertained people from around the world in this hall, and the cutlery was one way of her reminding them they were on Scottish soil."

"I'd be scared to use any of that stuff." Sandy muttered. "I bet it's all so valuable."

"It's either incredibly valuable or Graeme bought it from the supermarket last week and made up a nice story about it." Tom whispered. She let out a small laugh. It *was* hard to tell whether their tour guide was knowledgeable or imaginative.

"Now, if we can move our attention to the wall over here." Graeme said, moving the torch light on to the wall to Sandy's right. A huge tapestry hung on the wall, its colours muted with age. "This is one of my personal favourites. We have direct evidence that this tapestry was hung in this exact spot when Lady Margaret herself was in residence."

"What evidence?" One of the Americans asked, his voice high with curiosity. "I mean, surely, you didn't see a selfie on her Facebook profile with it in the background."

"No, no." Graeme said. "Lady Margaret preferred Twitter."

Sandy let out a snort of laughter.

"And then if we can look across to the left, I'll highlight some of the..."

"Ahhh!" It was Priscilla again. She let out a blood-curdling scream as the torch spanned across to the display case on the left. "Oh my, oh Lord no."

"What is it?" Graeme asked. Sandy heard movement among the group but remained still.

"Down there." Priscilla said through heavy tears. "On the floor, it's Marlene, she's... oh Lord. Oh Lord have mercy."

Graeme flashed the light across the floor, until Sandy saw the spotlight illuminate a figure on the floor. The group took in a collective gasp as they all spotted the shape.

"Marlene? Marlene, can you hear me?" Graeme called out.

Sandy watched the scene unfold with dread in her stomach.

The dagger in Marlene's back told her that Marlene wouldn't be responding to Graeme's questions.

6

_T_he scene was chaos.

Chaos in the dark.

Sandy watched as the flashlight remained on Marlene's lifeless body and her family wailed, lay down beside her on the floor, and demanded an explanation. Priscilla fainted.

Graeme attempted to ring for help but found, as Devon had earlier, that there was no phone signal within the castle.

"Someone needs to take charge." Sandy whispered to Tom.

"I have to get out of here." Priscilla, conscious again, cried. "Teddy, let's go."

"I'm not going anywhere." Teddy said. "I can't leave her."

"Well, I have to get some fresh air. My therapist says I can't be in high stress situations."

"Wait." Sandy said, the authority in her voice surprising nobody more than herself. "This is a murder scene. We're all witnesses. We can't leave until the police arrive."

"The police won't ever arrive if we can't get cell service." Devon said. Her voice was easy to pick out in the dark as her accent wasn't the same as the others'. She wasn't from the Deep South.

"Are you a cop?" One of the men asked.

"No." Sandy said. "I'm like a, a detective. A private investigator."

"Well you'd better investigate, then. Whoever did this to my mother needs to pay!" Teddy said, his voice catching on emotion.

"Graeme, I believe I can manage this situation until we can make contact with the police."

"Be my guest." Graeme said, eager to hand the responsibility over to someone else.

"Okay. Can I get everyone's attention? Graeme, move the torch, please. Thank you. My name is Sandy Shaw, and I'm going to be in charge until we can get help. I need everyone to stay calm."

"Calm?!" Priscilla shrieked.

"Graeme, we need a space where everyone can sit, and a small space where I can interview people individually."

"Interview? Woah, I know my rights, I won't speak without a lawyer." A young voice called out from the darkness.

"Enough." An older male voice chided.

"We can go to the drawing room. There's seating in there for visitors." Graeme said.

"Lead the way." Sandy said, her authority surprising her.

"Be careful, Sand. One of those Americans is a murderer." Tom whispered in her ear. Sandy felt a shiver run through her body as she realised he was right. She had dealt with murder cases before, but never in such a closed environment. She was in a party of ten, including herself and Tom, and one of them was a killer.

"Stay close together." She called as the followed the

light. She gripped onto Tom's hand and realised how grateful she was for the spooks she had felt earlier; they meant she could rule Tom out as a suspect straight away as he'd been holding her hand the whole time.

"Ok, this is the drawing room. You can sit on any chairs on this side of the roped area." Graeme explained as he switched off the torch. The drawing room had large windows that let in plenty of daylight. The room was divided into two sides by a thick velvet rope that marked the right-hand side of the room as out of bounds. The left side featured a row of chairs below the windows.

Sandy watched the tour party, eager to see their reactions in daylight. Priscilla had collapsed into a chair and was popping tablets from a foil pack, which she downed with a swig of bottled water. Teddy appeared disinterested in her dramatics, choosing instead to pace the length of the room. Sandy noticed huge damp patches around his armpits and on the back of his shirt, making it stick to his body.

Devon had an arm draped around Trixie, the other arm outstretched into the air as she attempted to get signal on her phone. She noticed Sandy watching her and shook her head.

"One of us needs to go outside to get service." She said.

Sandy nodded. "Tom, can you go out and call the police."

Tom looked at her carefully, reluctant to leave her in the presence of a killer.

"Please." She urged. She couldn't ask anyone else, and she didn't want to go herself and miss vital moments of assessing each person's reaction.

Jeff, the quiet son with the bald head, had taken a seat and was gazing blankly ahead into the distance. Curly-haired Eli, and his son Hamm, sat next to each other in silence.

And Graeme O'Connell appeared to be among the most jittery of the group. He stood by the velvet rope, as if guarding it from intruders, furiously biting the skin around his thumb nail. His left foot tapped rhythmically on the stone floor.

"I know you must all be in shock." Sandy addressed the group. She pulled her notebook and pen from her handbag. "But there's valuable information we need to gather right away. I need you all to give me some information about Marlene. What was her full name?"

"McVeigh." Devon offered. "Marlene McVeigh."

"And you're all related to her, is that right?"

Teddy nodded as he paced past Sandy.

The door at the far end of the room opened and Tom appeared. "Mainland police will come out as soon as they can but the waters are choppy, no boats are leaving Oban."

Sandy's heart sank. "There's no police on the island?"

Tom shrugged. "I got through to Oban. We need to sit tight until they can get across. They say a storm's coming in."

"Okay." Sandy said. "I'm going to gather some initial information and then start interviews. Nobody can leave this room, apart from coming with me for interview, until the police arrive."

"I have to be on a 10pm plane." Devon said.

"You're going home today?" Sandy asked the group.

"Just mum." Trixie said, her voice soft and quiet. The scared voice of a child.

"You'll be fine Trix, dad will be here." Devon said.

"You won't be on that plane." Sandy said. "The police won't let anyone leave until full interviews have been done."

"Look." Devon said. "What's happened here is clearly

awful, but I have things to do. I must be in the States tomorrow."

"Devon, please." Teddy said, his cheeks red and damp from his tears. "Your damn work will wait. Have some thought."

Devon's cheeks flushed.

"So, I think what we have here is Marlene's three sons, two daughters-in-law and two grandchildren. Right?"

It was Trixie who nodded.

"Are there any other relatives on this holiday?" Sandy asked, curious about the absence of the third daughter-in-law.

"No, this is all our family." Teddy said, then began to cry again. "This *was* all our family."

"It wasn't all my family." The teenage boy said. "You all think she's just disappeared since the divorce but she still exists."

"Your mum?" Sandy asked.

He nodded.

"Meghan and I divorced recently." Eli explained. "It's still very raw."

Sandy nodded and noted the name on her notepad. "Where is Meghan?"

"She lives in South Carolina."

"In a trailer." The teenage boy muttered.

"It's not a trailer, Hamm. Geeze, if your mom wants to live in a big house again she might have to go out and get a job."

"Hamm?" Sandy asked. "Is that your name?"

The teenage boy nodded. "She's got a job, dad. Unlike some people."

"I've had enough of your attitude!" Teddy shouted. He paced across to Hamm and glared in his direction.

"Leave him alone." Eli said. He rose to his feet and it was clear that he would be the winner if there was a fight. He was taller, with a more stocky build. Teddy shook his head and moved away, returning to pacing.

"Was there a special reason for this holiday?" Sandy asked.

"We have roots here." Teddy said, his voice unsteady from the confrontation. "Mom was tracing the family tree and wanted us all to come across here and see where we're from."

"Tom?" Sandy called. He walked closer to her. She whispered in his ear. "Go back outside and see if you can find anything out online about Marlene McVeigh."

He nodded and left the room.

"I'm going to start interviewing people one by one soon. Where would be a good space for that, Graeme?"

"There's a small room next door that the staff use as an office." Graeme said. He began to walk towards the door.

"Wait." Sandy called.

He spun on his heels and looked at her quizzically.

"Nobody leaves this room, that includes you."

"But..."

"No exceptions. Tom will watch everyone in here while I interview in the other room."

Silence descended across the room and Sandy returned to observing.

Trixie had begun to cry, her sobs muffled into her mother's chest as she clung to Devon, who rubbed her back and kissed her head. Jeff continued to stare into space ahead.

Eli and Hamm still sat together, their crossed arms mirroring each other, their expressions blank.

Priscilla had fallen asleep in her chair, a hand covered

her eyes and forehead as if she wanted to block out the world.

Teddy continued to pace, but had begun to mutter under his breath as he did.

The door opened and Tom reappeared.

He held up his phone, where he had taken a photo of an online news report for Sandy to see.

"Wow." She breathed as she read the headline.

"We have motive." Tom whispered.

7

"*T*eddy, come with me please." Sandy said. Her request stopped him in his tracks and his face blanched. "Everyone else, stay right here. Tom will watch everyone while I'm gone."

Tom eyed her anxiously but she chose to ignore him. Her stomach was sick with butterflies, but she ignored them and walked side by side with Teddy into the small office room.

The room featured a small desk with a chair at each side, and a computer that looked as old as the castle itself. She took the seat closest to the door and laid her notebook and pen on the desk. Teddy hovered near her.

"I'll need you to sit down, please." She commanded.

He did.

"I'm sorry for your loss." She said. "I can't imagine how hard it must be for you right now, but it's really important that we gather as much as we can to help the police. I'm sure you want the person who did this to be caught and punished."

Teddy shook his head and burst into tears again. "I can't

believe this has happened. I can't stop seeing her, on the floor…"

"Let's start with some easier questions. You're Teddy McVeigh?"

"Theodore. Everyone calls me Teddy."

"And Priscilla is your wife?"

He nodded.

"She's taking it hard. Was she close to your mum?"

"She takes everything hard." Teddy said. "She isn't very strong."

"Okay." Sandy said, making notes on her paper. Luckily, her handwriting was so bad she knew nobody else would be able to make out what her scribbles meant. "It's not cheap coming across here from America, you must have a good job I'm guessing."

"I have a great job." Teddy said with a smile. "It just doesn't pay any money."

"Oh?"

"I'm an artist." He declared. "I paint portraits mainly, watercolour but sometimes oils. I can do landscapes. I have to follow my muse, I can't just paint to order like some hacks do. The inspiration calls and I obey."

"How do you survive if that doesn't pay?"

Teddy smiled. "Oh, I have a generous allowance."

"Allowance?" Sandy asked. To her English roots, allowance meant pocket money. And Teddy certainly wasn't a kid. "What does that mean?"

"Oh!" Teddy exclaimed. "Two nations separated by a common language! Well, it's money from a benefactor, I suppose. Anyone who wants to support your work can give you an allowance so that you don't have to lower yourself and work in a cafe or something."

"Imagine that." Sandy quipped. "So you have a benefactor. Who is that?"

"My mother, of course." Teddy said. "She's my biggest fan."

"Okay. So your mum gave you a lump sum or regular payments?"

"An allowance every month." Teddy said. "It's not much, not when you think how much she has, but it let me focus on my painting."

"Your mum was wealthy, then?" Sandy asked, although she had already discovered that from the online article which declared her to the wealthiest woman in the state of South Carolina, and gave a motive for her to be killed.

"Oh she was more than wealthy." Teddy said, and his eyes glinted with an unreadable emotion. Envy?

"Does Priscilla work?"

"No." Teddy said. His voice faltered. "She's not really been very well."

"Oh, I'm sorry to hear that. What's been wrong with her?"

"She's such a delicate flower. And one day I'll be running for office, so she'll need to be at home to support me with that. It's probably not worth her getting a job."

"Office?"

"Politics, ya know? I've always wanted to make a difference to the world."

"Interesting." Sandy said. "Are you involved in politics now?"

"Goodness no, it costs so much money to run. I was waiting for my big break."

Sandy noted the past tense and wrote it down.

"Tell me about your relationship with your mum?"

"She's my best friend." Teddy said. "I tell her everything.

I only moved out because Priscilla insisted on it last year. I'd quite happily still be in the McMansion, eating breakfast on the balcony with her. It was a good life."

"The McMansion?"

"Oh!" Teddy said. "I forget we're not back home. Everyone knows the McMansion. That's what we nickname mom's house."

"It's a mansion, I take it?"

"Kind of. It's a plantation house. Here, I have some photos." Teddy said. He pulled his phone from his trouser pocket and flicked through images until he came to one, which he held up and showed Sandy. It was a beautiful three-level house with a green roof and a grand outdoor staircase leading to a wraparound balcony on the second floor. It was in the middle of a lush green lawn and nestled between what looked like cedar trees. It was certainly big enough to warrant the mansion nickname.

"That's beautiful." Sandy said.

Teddy shrugged. "Priscilla hates it. I don't know why she tried to compete with my mom, there was no need. She was never going to win."

Sandy nodded. "You two really were that close?"

"Of course. That woman did everything for me. She gave me everything I ever wished for. Aren't you close to your mom like that?"

The question stung and Sandy had to take a moment to compose herself. "My mum died when I was young."

"You poor girl." Teddy said.

"Thank you." Sandy said. "So, who do you think did it?"

Teddy sat back in his chair, distancing himself from the question. Sandy had planned to ask each person the same question, and at the point when they would least expect it.

"I don't have a damn clue." Teddy said.

"Really? There's no black sheep of the family?"

"The black sheep of the family? That's probably me." He admitted.

"In what way?"

"Not working, not practical like mom, no children. And I know the others talk. They talk about Priscilla."

"What do they say?"

Teddy took a deep breath. "She's an easy target, that's all it is. Devon's so detached from the family, so involved in her own life. And Meghan was too perfect for anyone to have a bad word about. But Priscilla, she doesn't have anything else to focus on. She has too much time, if you ask me. Time to create problems that don't exist and turn little arguments into huge problems. I mean, I'm the black sheep in the family, and she's never been accepted into the family."

"Does she know that?"

"Of course she does."

"Do you think your closeness to your mum has contributed towards that?"

"I know for a fact it has, but here's the thing Sandra. Is your name Sandra?"

"Sandy."

"Sandy, right. Here's the thing. My mom was the only reason Priscilla has that nose on her face. You know? So you can be jealous, or you can be grateful. And Priscilla doesn't know when to be grateful."

Sandy nodded, not sure what point Teddy was trying to make.

"She knows deep down she isn't half the woman that my mom is. I can't really argue with that. My mom, single parent, abandoned by our no-good daddy, builds a company and saves the day, every day. My wife, won't get out of bed some days."

"You said she's ill." Sandy reminded him.

"I say she's ill to strangers, it's an easier conversation." Teddy admitted.

Sandy thought of Priscilla, asleep in the other room. An outsider, a woman desperately jealous of her mother-in-law.

"What kind of relationship did your brothers have with your mum?"

"We're a very close family." Teddy said. "Everyone loves mom."

"Well, it would seem not everyone does." Sandy said. "Where were you standing when the lights went out?"

"Erm." Teddy's face blanched at the question. "I was right next to my mom. We had our arms linked together, we do that a lot. When the lights went out, we let go of each other in surprise."

"So you were the person closest to her. What did you do in the dark?"

"Nothing." Teddy said. He looked down at his hands, which were shaking in his lap. "I'm scared of the dark. I tried to reach for my mom again but I was scared of what I might touch in the dark. So I stood totally still and tried not to have a panic attack."

"Did you hear anyone move around you?"

"All I could hear was my heart beat thumping in my ears. I have this meditation technique I use before I paint, and I was trying that to calm my breathing but I was so scared."

"Did you hear the thud?"

Teddy shook his head. "I didn't hear anything until Graeme came back with the torch. I couldn't hear until I could see."

"Had there been any arguments recently among the family?"

"We're a family, we always have arguments. Nothing serious, though. Eli hasn't been happy for a while."

"The divorce?" Sandy prompted.

Teddy nodded. "It hit him hard. I think he still loves her."

"Should she have been coming on this holiday?"

"Erm, I don't really know."

"Okay. Is there anything else you want to mention?" Sandy asked.

"How much do you know about the tour guide?" Teddy asked.

"Nothing at all." Sandy admitted. "I'll question him like everyone else."

"It has to be him."

"What makes you say that?"

Teddy let out a long sigh. "Because he isn't family."

Sandy nodded. She remembered how awful it had been to consider that Tom had been capable of murder, and thought how devastating it would be to have to consider that a relative of hers could have killed. In a way she hoped Graeme was the killer too, because otherwise, the McVeigh family would not only be grieving, but would be torn apart by the crime.

"I'll speak to him." Sandy said, although she knew that he was the least likely suspect. He had no connection to the McVeigh family and no reason to murder a tour guest at random. Anyone who worked with the public knew that there were good and bad customers, but it was rare for a person to snap and kill someone who had simply annoyed them, asked one question too many, or stayed too long.

No, Graeme O'Connell was almost certainly innocent.

Marlene McVeigh had been brutally killed by one of her own relatives. A relative who had seen an opportunity when the lights went out, and acted in a quick and calculated way.

Could that person be Teddy, who appeared to dote on his mother?

Sandy remembered the flash of temper he had shown towards Hamm, a teenage boy who had just seen his dead grandmother's body. Not the actions of a loving uncle.

Could Teddy have the turbulent temperant of an artist?

"Teddy, I think you've helped me enough for now. Who would you suggest I speak to next?"

"How would I know?" Teddy said.

"You mentioned that Eli's had some issues. I think I'd like to speak to him next." Sandy said. Teddy showed no reaction to the suggestion. "Is there anything I should ask him about?"

"You're the private investigator!" Teddy said. He banged his fist onto the table, making Sandy jump. Her silly questions had worked. She had managed to see his temper. Quicker than she had expected.

"You have a temper, I see." Sandy said. She held eye contact with him as his cheeks flushed with colour.

"I am not the murderer." Teddy said.

"I never said you were." Sandy said, with a smile.

8

———

"*How* did he do?" Tom asked as Sandy returned to his side in the drawing room. The scene was almost identical to how she had left it. Teddy returned to his pacing without even a glance in his unconscious wife's direction.

"I'm not sure." Sandy admitted. "He seems like a real mummy's boy, but he was also living on her money and waiting for a big pay out so he can get into politics."

"You think the inheritance will be that pay out?" Tom asked, his eyes wide. "She certainly seems to have been wealthy enough."

"It's a possibility at least."

"The thing that bothers me is how quickly the murderer seized the opportunity. Who could be that calculated?"

"People will do anything if they're desperate enough." Sandy said. "I'm going to speak to Eli next, what do you make of him so far?"

"Nothing at all. He's sat out here with his son all the time, they haven't said a word to each other. He's not as whacked out as Jeff, that's for sure."

"Could be the cold and calculated person we're looking for?" Sandy asked.

"Who knows?" Tom admitted. He gave her a weak smile, clearly uncomfortable with his role in the investigation.

"I'd like to speak to Eli next, come with me please." Sandy called. Eli met her gaze and stood up. Hamm matched his movement and the two walked towards Sandy together.

She lead them back into the office, where Eli took the seat and Hamm remained standing.

"I really am sorry to be having this conversation." Sandy said. Eli nodded. Hamm gazed straight ahead at the stone wall. "Can you tell me a bit about your mum to start with?"

Eli sighed. "What do you want to know? Do you want to know about how she insisted on giving a generous maternity leave to her staff, or about how she started her company and still made it to every school show?"

"I guess I'd like to know who would have the motive to hurt her."

"Kill her." Hamm corrected.

"Kill her, yes, sorry." Sandy said, careful not to show a reaction to the words.

Eli shook his head. "That's all I've been thinking out there. One of my relatives is a killer. Somebody I love - even if it's pathetic Priscilla or ice-cold Devon, I love those women as much as I can't tolerate them - and one of them has taken our leader away from us all."

"And do you know why anyone would want to do that?" Sandy asked.

Eli was quiet for the longest time, and Sandy couldn't stand to look at his eyes. They were the deepest pool or sadness she had ever seen. For all of his external reaction, Teddy hadn't had that look of despair.

"Eli?" She prompted.

"No." He said finally. "I've got no idea."

"Tell me about the family dynamics. You're divorced?"

Eli nodded and glanced at Hamm. "My wife is a wonderful woman."

Hamm scoffed.

"It's the truth, son. Our marriage didn't work but I care deeply for Meghan. I always will."

"How was the divorce? Was it friendly, or..." Sandy asked.

"It was a train wreck." Hamm said. "The two of them trying so hard to act like best friends in front of me, as if I didn't know what was happening."

Eli pulled a face at Sandy. She could feel his discomfort and wondered whether to feel guilty for asking these questions in front of his son.

"I bet she's sad to have missed this holiday." Sandy said.

"She was heartbroken." Eli admitted.

"Is there anyone new in your life, romantically?"

"Oh no, absolutely not." Eli said. His eyes were earnest. She was warming to him more than she had expected to. Killers can be charmers, she reminded herself.

Sandy glanced at Hamm, who was staring at her.

"That's true." He confirmed.

"I understand that your mum was quite wealthy. Was she still supporting you financially?"

"Of course not." Eli said, then the hint of a smile crept up one side of his mouth. "Oh, you've spoken to Teddy. Yeah, she was paying his way, and hers - Priscilla's. But the rest of us work. I mean, Devon's earning the big bucks in their house, but Jeff and I weren't living on the bank of mommy."

"Okay." Sandy said. "What do you think about Teddy not earning his own money?"

Eli shrugged. "I don't pretend to understand artists. I work in finance, I'm a numbers guy. You give me an investment and I can tell you whether to throw your grandad's savings in it or not, and it's done me well. But I can't look at a picture and tell you if it's a masterpiece or garbage."

"That didn't really answer the question."

"I think a man earns his own living." Eli said, maintaining eye contact as he spoke. "I'd be grateful if you don't pass that on to my brothers."

Sandy nodded. The family had enough to deal with, without her stirring more problems.

"Tell me about Devon?"

"Not much to tell. She's here but she's not here. She's a scientist, she lives for her work. And Trixie, of course."

"She doesn't throw herself into family life?"

"We're not her family." Eli said. "She's made that pretty clear over the years. I don't know how mom managed to convince her to come on this trip. We're all here for two weeks, she flew in yesterday with us but she has a flight booked home tonight."

"Wouldn't it be Jeff who convinced her to come?"

Eli laughed. "Absolutely not. Have you spoken to Jeff? He won't say boo to a goose. He finds it physically impossible to say the word no. I mean, literally, he will not say that word. He's a people pleaser. So, if Devon said no - and trust me, she said no about this trip - he wouldn't have dared argue it."

Sandy jotted notes on her pad and let out a breath. "Would you say it's a happy marriage? Any jealousy from Devon towards your mum?"

"I'm clearly not the best judge of happy marriages, but there's no jealousy from Devon. She doesn't have enough interest in any of us to be jealous. She was pretty annoyed to interrupt her work to come out here, I heard her have a blazing row with mom before we all flew out."

"Tell me more about that?"

"We had a dinner the night before we flew, and Devon wasn't happy because she'd wanted her last night alone with Trixie to be quiet, just them, which I can understand, but mom insisted on hosting this fancy dinner at the McMansion. It was real good, ya know, fried green tomatoes, fried chicken, soft-shell crab, homemade peach pie. Mom really knew how to put on a dinner. So mom always asked the ladies to help her serve, and the men had to wash up after - it's always been that way. Started when we were little, mom would serve but the three of us would take it in turns to wash. So as the women have joined the family, they've helped serve and all three of us have split the washing. One washing, one drying, one putting away. Well, Meghan had decided not to come on holiday, so she wasn't there that night. And Priscilla was upstairs lying down because she was so scared about the flight. So it was just mom and Devon serving, and things got a bit heated."

"I need to know as much as you can tell me about the argument."

"Mom was accusing Devon of putting her work before her family, and that's when Devon said it. I mean, I've always known it, but Devon came out and said it. She said "you're not my family". I was going in the kitchen for some reason and it stopped me dead in my tracks. I mean, my mom has welcomed that woman with open arms, like she did Priscilla. She's looked after Trixie every time she's been asked, she's treated Devon like her daughter. I've had to comfort mom before about how Devon has been distant with her, and I've just said not everyone's as close as we are, but for her to come out and say that to her, it was a low blow."

"How did your mum react to that?"

"She leaned in real close and said to her, 'young lady, I'll be your family until the day I die'. I turned around and walked away then, and by the time they brought in the shrimp, nobody woulda guessed anything had happened."

"Wow." Sandy said as a chill ran down her spine.

"Yeah." Eli said. "Now, I like Devon, and I'm sure she wishes she could take those words back."

"Or she killed your mother." Sandy said.

Eli bit his lip. "Better that than my real flesh and blood."

"Let's talk about Priscilla." Sandy said.

"I'd rather not." Eli said, his gaze shifting.

"You've been very open so far, Eli. You've told me about your divorce, about you thinking Teddy should work, and all about Devon. Why don't you want to talk about Priscilla?"

The colour drained from Eli's face. "Because I'm not a detective, and I think you'll place too much weight on the answers I give you about her."

"What was Priscilla's relationship with your mom?"

"She hated her." Eli said. His voice shook as he spoke. "Priscilla couldn't stand her."

"Do you know why that was?"

"I could take a guess, but no, I've never sat down with her and asked her why she hated my mother. You should ask her."

"I will, but people are sometimes less than honest. You, for example, told me there's nobody in your life on a romantic level, but you have a love bite on your neck."

Hamm glared at his father, who had turned the colour of beetroot. The small red mark on his neck, just visible over the top of his shirt, could easily have been a birthmark or a bruise, but his reaction proves her suspicions were right.

Eli swallowed hard. "I'm not comfortable having this conversation with my son present."

"Why not, dad?" Hamm asked, his eyes fixed on the red mark. "I've already heard enough. I might as well know the rest."

Eli placed his head in his hands, and Sandy wondered if he was about to confess to an affair with Devon. Or Priscilla.

"I meant it when I said I still love Meghan." Eli said, his voice a whisper. "She dropped Hamm off the night before we flew but she forgot his passport, so I went across to collect it. We're adults, Hamm, and it hurts to be alone sometimes. I can assure you both that there's nobody in my life other than Meghan."

"Gross." Hamm said as he realised what his father was confessing.

"Sandy, I love my wife and I'm a good man. I wish our marriage had worked. Sometimes, outside influences get in the way of a happy ever after."

Sandy nodded. She knew that to be true. Her parents' own happy ever after had been cut far too short, and she had waited so long for her own happiness that she had begun to give up hope of happy endings ever being found.

"Eli, who do you think killed your mother?" Sandy asked. She expected that none of the family would answer this question with a direct answer, but she intended to ask them all.

Eli looked up and met her gaze. "I'm a numbers guy, like I told ya. If I was going to place a bet here, and look to get my money back, I'd have to say that Priscilla is the safest bet. I can also tell you that if I turn out to be right, my brother will be absolutely devastated. To lose his mom and his wife, I mean, that's more than any man should have to bear."

His voice caught as he finished speaking, and it was clear he was not only speaking about Teddy.

9

*S*andy allowed Eli a few moments to compose himself, then lead him back into the drawing room. Hamm skulked behind them, appearing to still sulk about the fact that his parents had hooked up.

Sandy watched as they returned to the same chairs they had sat on before the chat.

Tom had taken a seat near Graeme, and sat poker-straight.

"Can we have a word?" Sandy asked. He stood up and followed her away from the seating. "Are you ok?"

"Not really." Tom admitted. "I'm getting pretty spooked in here. I don't want to babysit these people. I'm going to go and chase up the police now you're back."

Tom practically sprinted out of the room towards the fresh air, where he'd be able to escape the others and get signal for his phone call.

Sandy sighed and looked at each person in turn.

Graeme watched her and when their eyes met, he rolled his eyes as if the whole incident was a dramatic waste of his time.

"I need a drink." A high voice called, and Sandy turned her gaze to see that Priscilla had woken up. She lay across a bench, the skin on her face and chest blotchy and red.

"There aren't any drinks." Graeme replied. "We're the only people here, there's no cafe!"

Priscilla sighed, but her eyes closed again immediately.

Sandy searched the room with her eyes for Teddy, to find him sitting by the far wall, his body curled into a ball.

Tom returned, his cheeks rosy from the cold temperature outside. "The boats are still not running. There's basically nothing they can do until the weather calms down."

Sandy gulped then plastered on a false smile. "It's down to us then."

Tom shook his head. "I'm out of my depth here, Sand. All I wanted was a quiet couple of days with you."

She took his hand in hers and gave it a gentle squeeze. "Me too. But that poor woman deserves justice, Tom, and I think I can work it out."

"Oh, I know you can work it out. You're amazing, Sandy Shaw." He said with a grin.

She flashed a smile at him, then addressed the others. "I'd like to speak to Jeff next. Follow me, please."

The first thing that happened when Jeff stood up was that he let out an awful howl, a primitive, mournful sound that Sandy at first thought was Lady Margaret's ghost arriving. The second thing was that he lost consciousness and fell, face first, onto the hard stone floor.

Eli was the first to dive to his assistance. He dragged Jeff into a sitting position, went in his man-bag where he had a bottle of water, and threw some in his face. Jeff became conscious within moments with a splutter. The First Aid technique had been unusual, but effective.

"Damn it Jeff." Eli grunted as his brother panted in his arms on the floor. "You scared the life out of me."

Sandy noted that Devon and Trixie watched the scene from their seats. She gave Jeff a few minutes to recover, then lead him into the office room, where he fell into the chair and immediately closed his eyes.

"Jeff, I'm really worried about you." Sandy admitted. The comment made him open his eyes and look at her. "I think you're in shock."

"Does that mean I'm not a suspect?" He asked. His voice was low and timid.

"Not necessarily. You could be in shock because you did it." Sandy explained. She had no basis for that theory but it seemed to make sense to her that a person could act in the moment and then go into shock afterwards, with regret.

Jeff gave her a panicked look. "I would never hurt my mom."

"I don't think you did." Sandy admitted. "But I'm going to find out who it was. Your mom deserves that, doesn't she?"

"Of course she does. She was my greatest role model. Everything I've achieved is because of her."

Sandy smiled at him. "And what have you achieved?"

The question seemed to puzzle him. "I have a beautiful daughter."

"What do you do for work?"

"I'm a manager of a supermarket."

"Okay." Sandy said, with surprise. She had assumed he was a house-husband when Eli had commented on Devon being the breadwinner.

"It's not glamorous or well-paid, but it's good honest work. I like it." Jeff said. "And with Devon gone so much at the lab, one of us needed to take a back seat."

"What did your mum think about that choice?"

"She supported every choice I've ever made."

"She didn't think a man should be the breadwinner?"

"Not at all. She's always been the breadwinner and she's raised us to know that men and women are equal."

"She must have got on well with Devon, since they're both strong, professional women."

"They didn't have the easiest relationship." Jeff said. "In fact, my mom struggled with all of our partners."

"Really?" Sandy asked.

Jeff nodded. "I don't know why. She made them very welcome, well, she made most of them welcome."

"But she didn't make Devon welcome?"

"Oh! She made Devon more welcome than Devon wanted to be. Her real issue was with Meghan."

"Eli's ex?"

Jeff nodded. "It's not my place to gossip about that."

"This is a murder investigation." Sandy said, the force in her tone surprising her and Jeff. "I need you to tell me about her problem with Meghan."

Jeff let out a long sigh. "Meghan had an affair."

"Oh, wow."

"Yeah. It was a one-off, with a work colleague. The thing is, Meghan had been the perfect daughter-in-law. Like, we would joke that there were four children, because Meghan and Eli were childhood sweethearts. Mom adored her. So, when it happened, Meghan told mom before Eli. She didn't know what to do."

"I'm guessing your mum told Eli?"

"Oh, she didn't tell Eli. She said it was family business and she arranged a family meeting. Everyone was there. Not Devon, she's never gone to a family meeting. But everyone else. And that's how Eli found out. Meghan told him she had had an affair and wanted a divorce."

"A divorce? Why would she..."

"Mom had told her there was no other choice." Jeff explained. "She felt so betrayed. I mean, she'd got Devon who was never going to really be that into family business, and then Priscilla who was constantly trying to one-up her, but she'd got the one perfect daughter-in-law. She couldn't stand the betrayal. Meghan had to leave the family."

"But surely that wasn't her decision to make?"

Jeff shrugged. "Eli was devastated, Meghan was devastated. Hamm went completely off the rails. And then, this trip was mentioned, and it was funny because mom and Meghan had always spoken about this trip - since we were teenagers. So mom decides to finally arrange it, and she includes Meghan in the eMail and books her a ticket, and it's like nobody dare mention it because she'd been cast out of the family by then - none of us could speak to her. The day before we leave, mom sends this eMail around saying she's made an awful mistake and included someone in the booking who isn't family."

"Meghan."

"Exactly." Jeff said as he shook his head.

"Did Eli want her to come?"

"Are you kidding me?" Jeff asked. "She's the only girl he's ever kissed. He worships the ground she walks on."

"That story doesn't make your mom sound too great." Sandy said. "Was it like your mom to be so harsh?"

"I wouldn't say she's the one in the story who looks bad." Jeff said. "Meghan had an affair, remember. Mom was standing up for Eli because she knew he was so in love with Meghan that he wouldn't see straight."

"Okay." Sandy said. "So, your mom was clearly very

involved in your lives still. How did Devon and Priscilla feel about that?"

"Devon really didn't say a whole lot about it." Jeff admitted. "She's very independent. I think, if anything, it amuses her. Priscilla found it a lot harder to handle. I think she saw mom as competition in some way. If mom was hosting a barbecue on Saturday, Priscilla would host one on Sunday and try and make hers bigger and better. Silly things like that."

"Do you think Priscilla had the motive to want your mom dead?"

Jeff pondered the question. "I couldn't say."

"So, it's not a no?"

Jeff squeezed the top of his nose between his fingers. "If you'd asked me yesterday if anyone wanted my mom dead, I'd have been more definite. Today, it seems someone did want her dead. And I don't know who that could be."

"How's your marriage, Jeff?" Sandy asked.

The change in questioning made Jeff release his nose and open his eyes wide. "I don't want to answer that question."

"That's fine." Sandy said. "The refusal to answer probably tells me everything I need to know. The people with happy marriages usually want to gush about them all the time."

Jeff winced. "The people who gush about the happy times are often the ones who can't survive the hard times. My wife and I are very different people, and we're very aware of each other's weaknesses. I believe we love each other, and we made a beautiful daughter together, and I'll take that kind of steady commitment over the highs and lows some people have."

Sandy nodded and allowed a smile to spread across her face. "I like that. I could go for that type of love myself."

"Well, the man you're with, he clearly loves you." Jeff said.

Sandy felt herself blush. "Oh, Tom, we're..."

Jeff shrugged. "He looks at you the way I used to look at Devon. Not like he fancies you - that's what you say over here, isn't it? Not like he fancies you, but like he sees your soul and is connected to it. It's a good way to love."

"You're very wise." Sandy said. She was stunned by how different the McVeigh brothers each were, and how much she had warmed to each of them in turn. "Your mother clearly taught you well."

"Ah." Jeff said, as a huge smile transformed his face. "She taught me that I could do anything in the world I wanted to do, and I've chosen to stay in the background and let my wife chase the glory. That's not an easy choice for a man to make, but I know my mom was proud of me for having the courage to make that choice, and I know my daughter and I have made some memories I'll cherish forever."

Sandy smiled. "Sounds good."

"Thank you."

"So, Jeff, who do you think killed your mom?" Sandy asked, the question not surprising Jeff as much as she had expected it to. He actually laughed in response.

"You're good!" He exclaimed. "Good cop, bad cop, all in one person. Okay, who do I think it was? I guess I have to take a guess?"

"Answer however you want." Sandy said.

"Hmm." He pondered. "I think it was Graeme O'Connell."

"Because he isn't family?"

"Well, there is that, but I worry that mom was too open

with people about her wealth. It caused unwanted attention at times. She always had pretend third-cousins twice removed asking for money. She even had a stalker once. She'd send personal eMails from the company account, and I told her not to because I knew the places she enquired would be raising the prices as soon as they realised who she was. I think Graeme McConnell saw that she was a rich lady and decided to kill her so he can sue her estate for the stress he'll have suffered."

Sandy took a moment to process the bizarre theory. "Why would he be so motivated by money that he would kill a stranger?"

"Gambling debts." Jeff said.

"You know that how?"

"I know how to spot a gambler. He acts just like my brother."

10

"*I* have a suspect." Sandy whispered to Tom. She had told the visitors to take a lunch break and they had all, to her surprise, obeyed. Each one had a backpack with pre-packed sandwiches, crisps and bottles of pop. Eli had an apple and what was left of his water after splashing Jeff. Priscilla had woken up and lay across Teddy's lap sobbing.

"Who?" Tom asked. They were the only ones without a packed lunch due to their last minute decision to do the tour.

"Teddy."

Tom raised an eyebrow but made no response.

"He did it for the money. He has no income, needs a big cash injection to launch his political career and, it turns out, he has gambling debt."

"Wow." Tom breathed. "Money can do awful things to a person. Would he really kill his mum, though? I mean, look at him, he's devastated."

"They're all devastated." Sandy said. "And it's only a

theory. I haven't spoken to everyone yet. Anything interesting happened out here?"

"I don't know." Tom said. "I keep thinking, how would I react if someone I loved was killed in front of me. I don't even know what would be strange behaviour in that situation."

"True." Sandy said. She thought back to the day she and Coral were told that their mother had died. Coral had wept, while Sandy had closed herself in her bedroom and felt her body grow numb. There were no tears, not until the funeral.

She gazed around the room at the family and realised they didn't look like one. They had lost their anchor and were drifting, separately, out to sea.

Teddy's face was soaked from silent tears that dripped from his chin onto his wife's hair. He seemed entirely unaware that she was there.

One thing was clear. Whoever had committed this act knew that Marlene McVeigh was central to the family and that their action would change the family forever.

"Priscilla?" Sandy called. The woman had made no attempt to eat so leaving her interview longer seemed pointless. "Can you follow me?"

Priscilla pushed herself off her husband's lap, then turned towards him. "No, honey, I'm fine, I'll do this alone."

Sandy frowned at her inappropriate sarcasm and lead her into the office room. She wondered if Priscilla would win her over like the others had.

"Priscilla, you seem devastated by what's happened. You must have been very close to your mother-in-law?" Sandy asked.

Priscilla rolled her eyes, which had grown bloodshot from all of her crying. "I couldn't stand her."

"They're strong words."

"Not strong enough. I hated her. I hated everything about her."

"Can you tell me why? What did she do to you?"

"She made it impossible to have a normal marriage, that's what she did. All three of them are as bad as each other, well, Eli's a little stronger, but Jeff and Teddy, they worshipped her. She said it's dinner at hers on a Friday, and it doesn't matter what plans I already had with my husband, it's dinner at hers. I've lived that way for years, being second best to her, and nobody else could see it."

"Does Teddy know how you feel?"

"Of course he does. And he will tell me to my face; he'll say, don't start this fight because you won't win. So basically, if he had to choose, he'd have chosen her, not me. It's the reason we don't have kids."

"How so?"

"I don't like being second best. Trust me, I have been a pampered princess my whole life, and I wanted a prince to come and rescue me and protect me. I've ended up with a man who will give me attention if his mother doesn't need him. But if I have a baby, it will be Marlene, then the baby, then me. And I refuse to go any lower than second place."

"Did Marlene want you to have children?"

Priscilla let out a breath. "Not really. She was very into women's rights, so to be fair to her, she wouldn't have ever put pressure on a woman to have a family."

"Okay. It sounds, Priscilla, like it was a fairly turbulent relationship between the two of you. That's a brave thing to come in and admit in a murder investigation, isn't it?"

"Oh please, our feelings for each other were pretty obvious. I'm sure everyone who has come in here has already told you what I have, why would I lie? At the end of the day, she was a woman who couldn't let her sons grow up, and now they're going to have to learn how to."

"You could say that her being killed makes your future look brighter?"

"If it doesn't send my husband completely insane, yes, I could say that." Priscilla admitted. Her honesty was startling.

"Are you happy she's dead?" Sandy asked.

Priscilla let out a small laugh. "I've dreamed about this day for years. The day when she's out of the picture and it's just me and Teddy to live our life. Who knows, maybe we'll be able to have a family, or move more than five miles away from the McMansion. We can be free to be husband and wife."

"Why the upset out there?" Sandy asked. "All of the tears?"

"I love my husband." Priscilla said as she twirled her wedding ring around and around her slender finger. "I can imagine how heartbroken he is today, and part of me has wondered if he'd be so upset if it was me killed, not her. That's an awful thought, you know."

"You've not been crying for her, have you?"

"I've never cried for that woman and I won't start now. I'm crying for myself, because she's out of the picture but she's still the only person he can see!" Priscilla shouted.

"His mother's just been killed, Priscilla. Surely you can understand."

"Maybe I've been too understanding for too long." Priscilla said. She crossed her arms and met Sandy's gaze. Her eyes were blank, emotionless. Sandy tried to disguise the shiver that ran through her spine.

"Did you kill her?" Sandy asked, hoping that Priscilla couldn't hear the shake in her voice as she asked the question. "Did you do this to get her out of the way so you could have Teddy to yourself?"

Priscilla laughed again. "Is that your theory? That I come in here and tell you exactly what my motive was, if I did it?"

"You haven't answered the question."

"The family would love it if it was me. They've wanted rid of me for years because I don't sit quietly like Devon does. Poor Meghan was as perfect as perfect can be and they still booted her out, and me? I just won't go. I keep turning up, day after day to help Marlene bake and run her around and take her lunch on busy days at work. I keep trying, even though I know I'm getting it wrong. I know that trying so hard is getting it wrong. But I can't stop myself. You know they say the way to a man's heart is through his stomach? Well, the way to my husband's heart is through his mother's."

Sandy pictured the dagger sticking out of Marlene's back. The dagger that, in the darkness, had managed to pierce Marlene's heart. She shuddered.

"You still haven't answered the question. I'll let the police know that you dodged that question and that you have a strong hatred for your mother-in-law." Sandy explained. She looked down and made notes on her pad, an opportunity for Priscilla to strike her. But Priscilla remained still in her chair.

"Is that it?" Priscilla asked.

"No, I have some more questions." Sandy said. "What was Marlene's relationship with the other relatives like?"

"She was loved by them all." Priscilla said. "Which doesn't make things look good for me, does it?"

"Even Devon?" Sandy asked. "If you're innocent Priscilla, you need to give me some information to help yourself."

Priscilla shrugged. "Let's say I did want her dead. Why would I do something here, where I'm the most obvious suspect? Surely I'd have done it back home, made it look like a break-in gone wrong or something?"

"That's a good point. But people snap under pressure, and maybe being on holiday together was the pressure that made you snap."

"Maybe." Priscilla said.

"So, about Devon?"

"Devon's just very detached from the group. She doesn't seem to care about what Marlene thinks, or thought. She leaves Jeff to do what he wants with the family, and she usually has work things that she does instead of joining in."

"Was there animosity between Devon and Marlene?"

"Oh no." Priscilla said. "Marlene was hurt by her sometimes, when she turned down invitations. Like she didn't want to come here. She'd give in occasionally, like she has now, to keep the peace a bit. But they didn't argue or anything."

"Someone told me they overheard Marlene and Devon arguing, that Devon told Marlene she wasn't her family."

Priscilla let out a gasp. "You're kidding? For real? Wow."

"That surprises you?"

"Not that she thinks it, I mean, that's obvious. It surprises me that she'd say it because Devon's a very mild person. I've never seen her temper. I think it's the scientist in her, you know? She's quite practical and logical. There isn't much emotion there. Maybe she's the one who snapped, hey?"

"Maybe." Sandy said, mirroring Priscilla's earlier answer. She took the lid off her pen and jotted Devon's name down.

"Anything else that I should know about the family dynamics?"

"You tell me." Priscilla said. "It's just a crazy group of people. And then you've got the ghost of Meghan in the shadows all the time, reminding me what might happen if I don't behave."

"You think Marlene would try to get rid of you?"

Priscilla shrugged her shoulders. "She's done it to one of us, I know she'd do it to me if I gave her cause. So I haven't given her cause. What that family did to Meghan is awful. She gave everything to this family, and she made one drunken mistake and lost everything. She's living in a tiny house now, has a job she hates because she left her job as soon as the kiss with her boss happened. Her whole life has been turned upside down. She worked so hard to get to where she was."

"I understand you don't work?"

Priscilla's cheeks flushed. "No, I don't."

"You manage to survive financially?"

"Yes." Priscilla said, her answer short and direct.

"Can I ask how? I know that Teddy has some, erm, expenses..." Sandy said.

"The gambling." Priscilla said with a sigh. "He was getting better for a while. Not that there was much incentive for him to stop when his mother appeared with whatever money he needed."

"She was bailing him out?" Sandy asked.

"Not exactly. He'd just ask her assistant for however much he needed, and it'd be in the account the same day. Marlene didn't ask what it was for."

"Can I ask how much roughly?"

"Well, there's $10,000 a month which is for our living expenses. I usually manage to stick within that budget unless it's like, ya know, birthdays or anything. I don't know what else Teddy asks for to go in his other accounts."

"Is it fair to say you don't know how much trouble he's in with debt?" Sandy asked.

Priscilla nodded. "And it's only going to get worse now."

"Worse? How?" Sandy asked.

Priscilla gave a smirk. "It's common knowledge so I think I can tell you. None of the family get a penny in her Will."

11

"*I*t's not Teddy." Sandy said as she regrouped with Tom after Priscilla's interview.

"Because his wife says so?" Tom asked with a smile.

Snady let out a small laugh. "No, because the family get nothing under her Will. That's his motive gone. He clearly adores her, his only motive could have been money. And, he was better off while she was alive."

"Back to the drawing board, then?"

"Not quite. Priscilla couldn't stand Marlene. She actually sat in interview and told me she hated her and dreamed about her dying. She dodged the question of whether she did it, too."

"You asked the most likely murderer if she'd done it?" Tom asked, his face ashen. "Geeze, Sandy, you have to be careful. Why don't I come in the interviews with you and Graeme keep watch in here?"

"We can't do that, Graeme's a suspect too."

"What? He didn't even know Marlene." Tom said.

"I know. It makes no sense, and I don't think it's him. But I have to speak to him. In fact, I'll do that next."

Graeme O'Connell sat alone, separate from the family, his legs crossed and his arms folded. *Stay away*, his body language seemed to imply.

"Graeme? Can I have a word?" Sandy asked. He jumped up, relieved to have something to do, and followed her into the office, where he took the seat she pointed to.

"Do you know who did it?" He asked.

Sandy shook her head. "Not yet. I'm still speaking to people."

"How can I help?"

"I need to ask you some questions, to exclude you from the investigation." She said.

"Oh, no." Graeme said. He stood up and backed into the wall. "You're not speaking to me as a suspect. No, absolutely not."

"Graeme, I have to speak to everyone."

"You don't have to do anything. You're not a police officer. You say you're some kind of detective but I've not seen any proof. I don't have to say a word to you."

"I will tell the police if you won't co-operate with me, and it won't look good on you. A murder has been committed on your watch, that already looks bad for you. There's going to be all kinds of investigations. You don't want it on record that you refused to co-operate to get justice for that poor woman."

Graeme sighed and returned to his seat. "Fine. I'll speak to you. But this is ridiculous. You can't possibly consider me to be a suspect."

Sandy remained quiet. She hadn't considered Graeme to be a suspect, but his unwillingness to speak made him seem suspicious. Maybe he did have something to hide.

"What can you tell me about how this booking was made?" Sandy asked.

Graeme stared at her. "Nothing at all."

"You don't remember a group of Americans booking a tour in advance?"

"I don't have anything to do with the bookings." He explained. "I shouldn't even be here."

"Where should you be?"

"Lord knows, but anywhere but here. I came out as a favour to my uncle, do a few shifts, that was all it was meant to be."

"How long ago was that?"

"Four years!" Graeme exclaimed. "Four years of my life wasted up here in the middle of nowhere."

"What happened to your uncle?"

"What do you mean, what happened to my uncle?"

"You were coming to cover a few of his shifts?"

"No!" Graeme said with a laugh. "Not his shifts, heck no. He doesn't work here, he owns the place."

"I see." Sandy said. "So, what exactly do you do here?"

"I'm a tour guide." Graeme said. "I thought I'd made that clear."

"You don't do anything behind the scenes?"

"I am a complete and utter dogsbody, I do whatever's needed."

"Is it just you here? No other staff? Where does your uncle live?"

"He lives on the mainland, he never comes here. Well, if there's a newspaper article or something, he'll come and pose for a photo. But yes, it's just me. I've been threatening to leave ever since I came, but nobody wants to replace me."

"You're not happy here?"

"I'm downright miserable." Graeme admitted. "I don't know anyone. I came up here as a favour, and I needed the money."

"Were you in trouble?"

"I got myself into a spot of bother, yeah. Started out as a poker night with mates, just once a week or so. Then I thought I'd practice online. Lost my mum's life savings on there. That's when my uncle said he could offer me some work here, give me a chance to repay my debts."

"Wow." Sandy said. "Are you still gambling?"

Graeme shook his head. "Never again. I had to sit my mum down and tell her it had all gone. Worst feeling in the world. I think I got a bit addicted to it all, her face stopped all of that straight away."

"How much was it?"

"£500." Graeme said, with a sad smile. "I paid her back but it's not the same. She'd scrimped and saved all her life to get that £500. I could give her ten times that if I had it and it wouldn't matter, it wouldn't be her five hundred back."

"So you had no idea a wealthy American was coming on today's tour?"

"I get to work and check the list. They're just names to me. Are you suggesting I killed her because she had money? That would make no sense."

"I'm just exploring options." Sandy said.

"I've got access to money." Graeme said.

"Your uncle?"

He nodded.

"Forgive me, but if your uncle has money, why were your mum's savings so small?"

Graeme scratched his nose before he answered. "The money's on my dad's side. He screwed her over pretty well when he left. They were never married."

"I see." Sandy said. "So, what do you make to all of their reactions out there? Anything strike you as being curious?"

"Nah." He said. "They're all probably in shock right now,

aren't they? Apart from the killer. So, my bet's on whoever's acting most normal."

"And who do you think that is?"

"The New Yorker. She's more bothered about her flight tonight."

"She's certainly pretty detached from it all." Sandy said.

"She's not detached, she's exactly as she was before it happened." Graeme explained. "Before you two arrived, she was off to the edge of the group, on her phone all the time, making it clear she couldn't be late for her plane. It's not as if her response to the murder is to go within herself, she just hasn't shown a reaction at all."

"That's interesting." Sandy said. "Anything else?"

Graeme shrugged. "There is one thing actually. One of the family didn't turn up for the tour today."

"What?" Sandy asked. Graeme put a hand in his trouser pocket and pulled out a neatly folded sheet of paper, which he passed across the desk to her.

"Here, take a look."

Sandy read the sheet, which was the guest list for today's tour. All of the family names were listed together with phone numbers, and underneath Eli, was Meghan.

"You know who she is?" Graeme asked.

"I do." Sandy said. "Thanks for this, can I keep it?"

Graeme shrugged. "I usually mark each person off as they leave at the end but I can't imagine I'll need to do that today. Sure, keep it."

"Thank you." Sandy said. She studied the sheet of paper, focused on the one person who she hadn't met. Meghan McVeigh. Could she be a suspect? "Let me walk you back."

Sandy left Graeme in the drawing room and walked through the grand space and out the nearest door. She stood in the castle grounds, where she was reminded how bitterly cold the day was. Sheets of wind smacked her body, forcing her to take shelter underneath an archway that cut through the castle.

She took her phone out of her pocket and dialled the number, taking care to remember the correct code to allow her to make an international call. The dial tone told her she had done it right. It was only just lunch time in Scotland, which meant it would still be early morning in South Carolina.

Finally, after several rings, the line was answered.

"Hello?" Came a lilting Southern accent.

"Is that Meghan McVeigh?"

"It is. Who's calling please?" Meghan asked.

"My name is Sandy Shaw. I'm calling from Scotland. I'm here with your son and your husband."

"Are they okay? What's happened?" Meghan asked.

Sandy didn't have questions prepared for Meghan. The fact that she had answered a call on her landline proved her innocence. She didn't want to share the news of Marlene's murder, but had little choice. "They're both fine, but something awful has happened and I was hoping I could ask you some questions."

"Sure." Meghan said. Her voice was so friendly, so pretty and All-American. Sandy could imagine her being the perfect daughter-in-law.

"I want to ask about your relationship with Marlene McVeigh."

"What's she done?"

"She hasn't done anything. She's dead, Meghan. She's been killed."

The line was quiet for several seconds, then a sob broke the silence. "Oh Lord, please no."

"I'm so sorry to have to tell you this."

"Are you with the police?"

"I'm investigating until the police arrive." Sandy explained.

Meghan took a deep breath. "I'll tell you whatever you need to know."

"Why aren't you here, Meghan? Your place was booked." Sandy asked.

"That was cruel." Meghan said. "I tried to rise above it, but it was a cruel trick. Not just for me, but it was cruel for Eli and it was cruel for Hamm."

"Are you saying Marlene booked you the ticket with no intention of you coming?"

"I can't prove that, but Marlene isn't a lady who makes mistakes. She's very meticulous. She knows how to book a holiday. I was very upset by that."

"Would you have come?"

"If I was wanted, of course." She admitted. "I love my husband."

"I know you made a mistake... an affair?"

"Affair?!" Meghan exclaimed. "Is that what they're saying?"

"Tell me what happened."

"It was a kiss. I know that's bad, I'm not making any excuses, but I'd been drinking and so had he. He was my boss. I'm not going to say I didn't have a choice, but I don't stand up to authority very well, and I was so surprised. When he kissed me, I panicked and I kissed him back. That was it."

"And you and Eli couldn't work it out?"

"I guess not." Meghan said.

"I'm pretty sure he still loves you." Sandy said.

"Oh, I know." Meghan said. "And I love the bones of him, I really do. But Marlene wouldn't let him take a chance on me after that. You know her husband cheated on her? She took him back the first time, and then the second time he fell for the girl and ran off with her."

"Marlene didn't want Eli going through the same thing."

"Exactly." Meghan said. "And I have to respect that. I mean, I'm a mom too. I wouldn't want to see Hamm get hurt like that. Sandy, can I ask you something?"

"Of course."

"What happened? I mean, do you know who did it? Is everyone else safe?"

"Nobody else is in danger." Sandy said. She hoped it was the truth. "I can't say much more at the moment. Don't try to contact anyone, we're going through speaking to people now so nobody can make or take a call."

"Thank you for letting me know." Meghan said. "Please look after my boys. I love them so much."

And with that, Meghan ended the call, leaving Sandy alone in the fierce wind.

12

"*A*ll okay?" Tom asked when Sandy returned to the drawing room. Her fingers were red raw from the cold. She squeezed them into fists but the movement was painful.

"Yep." She said. "I just spoke to Meghan, Eli's wife."

"And?"

"She answered the phone at home in South Carolina, so she's not a suspect."

"You're thorough! That hadn't even occurred to me!"

"I didn't think it was likely, but at least we know."

"What's she like?"

"She sounded really nice. Really normal."

"Still think it's Priscilla?"

"I don't know." Sandy admitted. "Surely if she did it, she'd try to hide how much she hated Marlene?"

"Maybe." Tom said with a shrug. "But sometimes hiding in plain sight is the best protection. I mean, you're doubting her guilt now precisely because of how strong her motive was."

"That's a really good point." Sandy said. She looked

across at Priscilla, who was asleep again. "And everyone else had already told me about her problems with Marlene, which she would guess they'd have done. She had to either admit it, or lie."

"And those little lies cause big problems." Tom said.

Sandy turned to him with a grin. "Listen to you, Detective Nelson! You're getting into it!"

"It's hard not to. I want to know who did it and why. I just want you to be safe."

"I know." She said. She stroked the side of his face, her fingers brushing through his stubble. "Thank you."

"I guess you want to speak to me?" A voice came from behind Sandy and she dropped her hand quickly. She turned to see Devon standing a few feet away, her arms folded across her chest.

"Yes, I do. Follow me." Sandy said. She flashed Devon a smile and tried not to feel intimidated.

"My daughter can come in with me." Devon said. Her tone told Sandy it wasn't a question.

"Of course." Sandy said. Trixie hadn't left her mother's side since Marlene's body had been discovered in the darkness of the banquet hall, and to Sandy's surprise, when Devon took a seat, Trixie sat on her knee.

"Okay, let's get this over with." Devon said.

"Devon, the scientist." Sandy began. "Everyone's told me how much you love your work. Was it hard for you to take this time out?"

"I'm back home tonight." Devon said. "I need to get cell service so I can add on a seat for Trixie."

The teenage girl nestled into her mother, which was difficult given her long and leggy frame.

"You don't want to stay with your dad, Trixie?" Sandy asked. The girl shook her head but said nothing.

"Do you know when the police will be here?" Devon asked.

"I don't." Sandy said. "Hopefully soon. Can you tell me about your relationship with Marlene?"

"She was my mother-in-law." Devon said.

"Were you close?"

"No."

"Did you like each other?"

"We weren't friends, Sandy. I married into her family."

"So it wasn't a close relationship." Sandy said. It was hard work, extracting information from Devon.

"No."

"Your husband, he was close to his mother?"

"Very." Devon said.

"Did that bother you?"

"No."

Sandy paused, waiting for Devon to fill the silence. She didn't.

"It didn't bother you at all?"

Devon cracked her knuckles and sighed. "Why would it? It really wasn't my business how close Jeff was to her. I had better things to worry about."

"Like your work?"

"Yes."

"What do you do exactly? I know you're a scientist."

"That's right." Devon said.

Sandy took out her notebook and scribbled notes that Devon wouldn't be able to read, while watching to see if her action caused any response. It didn't. Devon was cool as a cucumber. Sandy didn't like her.

"Who do you think killed Marlene?"

Devon shrugged.

"You have no idea?"

"No."

"Devon, I understand that you want to get your plane sorted, but I need people to be open with me so I can solve this case."

"Okay." Devon said, but her demeanour was unchanged.

"How would you describe yourself? Is this the real you, sitting there? You seem detached."

Devon smiled. "I am detached."

"Okay... why?"

"I always have been."

Sandy glanced at Trixie, who had closed her eyes and placed her thumb in her mouth.

"How old is your daughter?"

"Sixteen."

"Did she get on with her grandmother?" Sandy asked. She expected the focus on Trixie would force emotion from Devon.

"Trixie?" Devon prompted.

"Yeah, I love her, she's great." Trixie said without opening her eyes.

"Well, if you don't have anything else to add, I'm done."

"Thanks." Devon said. Trixie stood up and then Devon did, and they walked out of the room in front of Sandy, their arms linked together.

Sandy returned to Tom's side.

"Well, if we're looking for a cold, calculated killer, it's Devon." Sandy said. "I can't read that woman at all. I don't know if she just doesn't care, or well, just really doesn't care."

Tom gazed past Sandy and a smile crept onto his face. She followed his gaze.

Devon and Trixie were curled into each other, and it

looked as if Trixie had fallen asleep. Devon stroked her hair and planted a kiss on her forehead.

"I know what you're thinking." Sandy said.

"Yeah, she doesn't look cold or calculated."

"Maybe she really is just uninterested in the McVeigh family."

"Could be." Tom said. "Look, I'm going to chase the police again. I can't believe they're not here yet."

Sandy nodded at him as he walked through the drawing room and out of the castle. It was nearly 1pm.

She had interviewed all of the suspects.

And she had no idea who the murderer was.

All she knew, as she stood by the velvet rope and faced the chairs, was that she was standing in the same room as the killer and that the police were in no rush to come and keep the rest of them safe.

She jumped as a huge bolt of thunder roared across the sky, causing the lights to flicker.

She swallowed a gulp and hoped that Tom would return quickly.

13

"*E*veryone listen." Sandy called to the group. "The police are still not on their way. They can't physically get here until the weather improves. So we all need to sit tight and wait. If anyone wants to speak to me again, with new information, just let me know."

"Can I go and make a call now?" Devon asked.

"No, nobody can make a call or leave this room." Sandy said.

"You can't keep us trapped in here." Devon said. She stood up, gently moving a still-asleep Trixie. "I'm not a prisoner. I'm going to stand outside and make some calls."

"Devon." Sandy said. "You won't be on a plane tonight. So if you want to go and book an extra seat, there's no point."

"I can't miss my flight." Devon said.

"Will you listen to yourself? Our mother has been killed and you're worrying about work as normal!" Teddy shouted, from his foetus-like position on the floor.

"I wouldn't expect you to understand." Devon muttered under her breath.

"I understand plenty!" Teddy exclaimed. "And I know when someone's priorities are wrong."

"Teddy, you need to calm down." Devon said. "I'm going to make that call now, Sandy."

"Go with her." Sandy told Tom, who nodded and followed her out of the room.

"Don't talk to my mom like that." Trixie said. She must have been disturbed when Devon stood up. "She doesn't deserve it."

"I'm sorry Trix." Teddy said. "We're all just upset."

"This family don't respect our mothers." Hamm said. He had folded a sheet of paper into a ball and threw it into the air repeatedly, catching it then tossing it up again.

"Now isn't the time." Eli said, his voice low.

"It's never the time." Hamm said. He stood up and moved away from his father, taking a seat next to Trixie, who despite being a year older was much smaller than him. She offered him the weak smile of a nervous ally.

"Can we get out of here yet?" Priscilla asked, awake. She lay prone on a bench. Her constantly startled eyes had taken on a mad look. "This place is too cold."

It was true. The heating system installed in the castle was adequate for the length of the tour, but the large spaces were too cold to spend hours in. The small office room was warm, but the public spaces were chilly.

All of a sudden, Devon reappeared with Tom at her heels.

"The police are on their way." She called to the group. She noticed Trixie sat next to Hamm and raised an eyebrow. Trixie stood up and moved to an empty seat, and Devon took the seat next to her.

"Excellent. Thank you." Sandy said. "Let's sit tight, the police will be here soon."

"I wish we'd never come here." Eli said. The group murmured their agreement.

"I can't believe she's gone." Jeff said. "She talked about coming here and tracing the family tree for so many years, and she never got chance."

"She was only here now to prove a point." Eli said.

"What?"

"Oh come on, this whole holiday was planned by her to show Meghan what she'd lost." Eli said. His voice was matter-of-fact but his foot tapped the stone floor furiously as he spoke.

"Watch what you're saying." Teddy said. "It was mon's dream to come here. It's not her fault your wife looked elsewhere."

Eli dropped his head into his hands and let out a low scream of frustration.

"Dad?" Hamm asked. He moved across the room and placed an arm around his father.

"I've lost them both." Eli whispered and descended into tears.

Sandy watched the scene unfold. She noted how Devon remained at the periphery, not offering comfort or criticism to anyone, focused only on Trixie. She saw how Priscilla increased her own display of emotion whenever another person seemed to compete for the position of chief mourner. And she saw how Teddy, whose entire income source had just disappeared, rocked back and forth slowly on the floor.

"Can I go back to the banquet hall?" Teddy asked, his voice wavered as he spoke.

"No, we can't allow that." Sandy said. "It's a crime scene."

Teddy nodded and began to cry. "She shouldn't be alone in there."

Sandy watched him in his grief and felt a lump form in her throat. "I'm sorry, Teddy. All of you, I'm sorry this has happened. I can't imagine what you're all going through."

She made eye contact with Hamm and saw how young he looked, the child behind the cool, baseball-capped exterior. "I spoke to your mum, Hamm. She sends her love."

"You spoke to my mom?" He asked. The colour drained from his face. "Is she okay?"

"She's fine. She sends her love to you. And you, Eli."

Eli's cheeks flushed at her words, and he smiled and nodded in her direction. His eyes were full of uncried tears.

"If only she was here." Jeff said.

"Don't you dare!" Hamm cried. "You turned your back on her. All of you did."

"What did you mean, Jeff? If only she was here?"

Eli took a deep breath. "She's a trauma nurse. I imagine he means that she may have been able to help."

Jeff nodded. "She's a fine nurse. I'm sorry, I didn't mean to upset anyone. I know emotions are running high."

"Jeff, there was no saving your mum." Graeme said. HIs voice surprised Sandy. He had said little throughout the time since Marlene was killed and, as often happens, the sparsity of his words made them seem authoritative.

"He's right." Devon said. "She would have died instantly."

Jeff bit his lip and nodded his head. Up and down. Up and down. Sandy turned away after a full minute, not wanting to watch any longer.

"Devon just rang the airport?" She asked Tom.

"And the police."

"Did she book another seat on the flight?"

"Yep. Bumped them both into First Class. Economy was full."

Sandy shook her head. "She just won't listen. The police will need statements from everyone, there's no way any of us are going far today."

"She just wants to be in control." Tom said. "I know you have your suspicions about her but I like her. I like her more than Priscilla anyway. She's acting as if she's the big victim here, and yet she can't stand the woman who was killed. And, her husband is devastated, and she hasn't shown him one bit of sympathy. The only time she went close to him was so she could collapse in his lap."

"You'd rather a cool, practical woman?" Sandy asked with a cheeky grin.

"If they were the two choices, absolutely."

"Tom, you're a genius." Sandy said. He eyed her quizzically. "You've given me an idea."

14

*T*he mainland police arrived as the sky grew dark. The storm had retreated and only the usual sound of the wind blowing outside could be heard through the thick castle walls. The noise was reassuring to Sandy.

The castle's position atop a hillside, just like Waterfell Tweed's own elevated location, meant that wind was to be expected.

They burst into the drawing room, six male officers and three female officers, dressed in full riot gear as if they were attending a hostage situation.

"It's okay." Sandy said, holding her arms up in the air. "Everyone's here, present and accounted for."

The officers slowly relaxed and removed their helmets.

Priscilla had fallen asleep again, and so had Trixie, who was curled up against her mother's slender frame.

After the lively discussion earlier, the group had fallen silent, each person focused on their thoughts. Sandy had taken the chance to watch them in turn and develop her theory.

"What happens now?" She asked the male officer who appeared to be taking the lead.

"We need ta take ye all in for questioning." He said through a thick Scottish accent.

"I've already interviewed all of the suspects." Sandy said.

The officer began to laugh. He had a thick white moustache and looked a little like a walrus. "Including yoursen, ave ye?"

"Well, no." Sandy stuttered. She hadn't expected this response. "I know I didn't do it."

"S'what they all say." He said. "Ye police?"

"No, but I do investigate murders. I've solved three." Sandy said. She tried to remain confident. "I knew it was important to speak to people quickly, and separately, so I set up a makeshift interview room and I can give you a summary of that information."

"Ah. Well, lassie, we'll tell ye if we want it." He said. He coughed up some phlegm into his hand and reached into his pocket for a grotty handkerchief, to which he added the phlegm, before addressing the group as a whole. "Listen up, we'll be moving ye across soon."

He moved past Sandy as if they hadn't spoken a word to each other before, and headed out of the room towards the banquet hall. Sandy began to walk after him until a hand gripped her arm and stopped her. She turned to see a female officer.

"You have to stay in here." The woman explained.

Sandy let out a sigh. She had been transformed from investigator to suspect. Or witness at least. "There's no lighting in the room where Marlene is. I wanted to tell him he'll need a torch."

"He's got it covered. You need to stay here with everyone else."

Sandy nodded and took a seat next to Tom. "I can't believe I didn't see this coming."

"What do you mean?"

"We're suspects now! I imagined the police would arrive, I'd explain what had happened, and they'd thank us for our help."

Tom smiled across at her. "They just need to secure the scene to start. You know, it's pretty amazing really."

"What is?"

"Everything they're doing, it's the things you did. I mean, Graeme was pretty clueless, which is fair enough. When you're a tour guide you don't expect to have to handle a murder. But you sprung into action and did the right things. Don't beat yourself up because you haven't found out who did it."

Sandy bit her lip and looked up at him.

"What does that look mean?" Tom asked.

"Wait and see!" Sandy said, with a wink.

The officer with the thick accent returned to the room and gestured to two of his colleagues. They stood close together by the doorway and he whispered to them. He caught Sandy's eye at one point but blanked her. When he finished speaking, the two officers nodded at each other and walked out of the drawing room towards the banquet hall.

"Ladies and gentlemen, thank ye for your patience. We have some work to do here gathering the evidence and then we'll all leave together."

"Will you be taking us to the mainland?" Devon asked, her mind no doubt focused on her flight time.

"No." He said. "We'll be using a station here on Mull. You'll all be interviewed. It's going to be a long night. Now, who do we have here? Names, please."

He went down the group one by one, each person providing their name.

"Stay awake now, lasses." He said, with a glance towards Trixie and Priscilla. "Surprised ye can sleep after what's happened."

"We flew in from America yesterday. We're all pretty jet lagged." Eli explained. Was he the new head of the family, Sandy wondered, now that Marlene was gone.

"Well, I'm advising ye to stay awake and alert. One of ye is a murderer, after all."

Sandy flinched at the officer's blunt words.

"Excuse me?" She said. She stood up and the officer looked at her in a way that suggested more exasperation than curiosity. "I believe I can save you and your colleagues a great deal of work. I know who the murderer is."

A gasp came from the group, but Sandy was focused only on the police officer, her steely stare daring him to object.

"A confession is it?" He asked.

"No." Sandy said. "I'm being serious. Will you give me ten minutes?"

"I don't think that's a good idea." The officer said. He looked past her in the direction of the banquet hall, where several of his colleagues had gone to secure the scene.

"Please." A voice came.

Sandy turned to see Teddy. He was up off the floor and stood near her, his face pained.

"I want to know what happened. If you think you know, I'd like to hear it." Teddy said.

The officer shrugged. "I can give ye ten minutes."

"I need everyone's attention." Sandy called. Priscilla rubbed her eyes, her mascara trailed across her cheeks. Eli cleared his throat and placed his hand in his son's.

Devon glanced at her watch, met Sandy's gaze, then returned the movement and checked her watch again.

"Teddy, it's interesting to me that you are so keen to know what happened." Sandy began. She had never addressed a crowd at such a momentous occasion and felt sick with nerves. "You were my first suspect."

Sandy watched as the colour drained from Teddy's face.

"Me? I adored my mother." Teddy said.

"Adored her too much." Priscilla spat from her seat.

"It's an interesting dynamic to me, your relationships with your mother and your wife. You certainly seemed devastated by her death. But, then, so did everyone else, and yet one of you killed her. I know that lots of you wanted the killer to be myself, or Tom, or Graeme, so it wasn't a family killing. But I know it wasn't me, and I was holding hands with Tom all the time the lights were out so I know it wasn't him."

"And Graeme? How much does anyone know about him?" Teddy asked, his voice high-pitched. He had resumed his frantic pacing.

Graeme sat at the far edge of the group, close to Tom. He shook his head slowly. "I know it would be a hundred times easier for you all if it was me, but it wasn't. I'm not a killer, and I had no reason to want to hurt Marlene. She seemed like a nice lady."

"A rich lady!" Teddy shouted.

"So surely I'd want to keep her alive and hope for a nice big tip at the end of the tour?" Graeme said. He glanced at Sandy then. "Sorry, that sounded more flippant than I meant. It doesn't matter how rich or poor she was, I had no reason to want her dead."

"He's right." Sandy said. "I did consider any motive he might have, I assure you all. But I think you know deep down that you were hoping it was one of us outsiders, because you couldn't stand to think it was one of you."

"Are you saying it was Teddy?" Eli asked. "Because, that's absolute nonsense. We all loved mom but nobody was closer to her than Teddy."

"As I was saying, the dynamics interested me. You clearly loved your mum, but you were in need of a large cash injection - to begin your political career and pay off your gambling debts."

"But..." Teddy began.

"Then I learnt that none of you stood to benefit under Marlene's Will. And that changed things completely."

Sandy had the group's attention completely. Even Priscilla looked somewhat alert.

"When a wealthy person is killed, the obvious motive is always money. And I've learnt that the obvious things in a murder case can be a distraction from the more subtle clues. I've spent a lot of time sitting back and watching you all interact as a family. We have three devoted sons, and each son has paid the price for their devotion. Eli, your marriage has been lost. Jeff, you're immersed in a biological family that your wife doesn't want to be consumed by. And Teddy, you've deliberately chosen your mum over your wife at every opportunity."

"Finally." Priscilla said. "Someone sees the truth."

"That's why my investigation highlighted you, Priscilla."

"What?" Priscilla asked, her plumped-up lips open in surprise. "That's insane!"

"You hated Marlene. You told me as much. You hated being in her shadow, and Teddy had made it clear that you'd stay in her shadow as long as she was around."

Priscilla looked across at Teddy, who had begun to sob.

"I had my problems with her." Priscilla said. "Maybe I

was a fool to be honest about them with you, but I'm not a liar. And I'm not a murderer."

"You're right." Sandy said. "And it was your honesty in interview that helped you, actually. You hated her, but your hate is misdirected. What you actually hate is your place within this family, and that was down to Teddy, not Marlene."

Teddy walked over to Priscilla and sat on the floor in front of her, where he buried his head into her. "She's right." He said, through choked sobs. "It was me. I didn't appreciate you."

Priscilla began to cry and wrapped her arms around her husband. Sandy felt her cheeks flush and looked away.

"Priscilla's emotion made her a suspect, while Devon, your lack of emotion made you a suspect."

Devon gazed up at Sandy and nodded her head. Trixie clung to her side.

"It's okay." Devon murmured to her.

"You also had the most obvious motive to choose now to strike. Your argument with Marlene the night before your flight was overheard."

Devon gave a sad smile. "I regret those words."

"Marlene told you she would be your family until she died. And just hours later, she's dead. You've shown none of the compassion that the others have, and to say that you're a scientist is, I think, unfair to scientists. You've been cold and distant."

"Devon?" Jeff asked from across the room. His face was stricken with concern.

"Surely, only a killer would have such a detached reaction."

Devon nodded. "We can finish this at the police station, I think."

"Mom?" Trixie asked, as she pulled on her mother's face to force her to meet her gaze.

Jeff stood and walked across the room, where he mirrored Teddy's position by kneeling on the floor in front of Devon and Trixie.

"What have you done?" He asked. He cupped Devon's face with his hands and pulled her towards him.

"Do you want to tell him, or shall I?" Sandy asked.

Devon closed her eyes and waited, braced herself for what Jeff might do.

"Okay. I'll explain." Sandy said. "Devon, you're practical and logical. While everyone else has been taken over by emotion and grief, you've remained practical. You've been watching and thinking. I watched you watch them."

Devon opened her eyes and looked at the officer with urgency. "I think we've said enough. You can take me to the station now."

"We can't leave until they've finished in there, lass. Sit tight." The officer said.

Eli looked across the room towards Devon. "It was you?"

Devon stared straight ahead.

"For a cold-hearted killer, you're exceptionally close to your daughter." Sandy said. Trixie looked at her with big doe eyes. "The one way I've seen emotion from you is toward her. You love her."

"Of course I do." Devon said.

"You want her to have a bright future."

"Of course." Devon said. Her composure had started to crack and her voice wobbled.

"And you do care for this family, even if you aren't as involved as they'd like you to be."

Devon didn't answer.

"That's why you're willing to take the blame for a crime you didn't commit." Sandy said.

The group gasped. Devon shook her head and began to cry.

"You worked out the truth even before I did, didn't you? And you calculated your reaction to bring suspicion on yourself." Sandy said.

"Mom, why would you…"

"Shh, darling, shh." Devon said. She grabbed Trixie and held her tight.

"There's a person who is central to this case, and she isn't even here." Sandy said, assessing the reactions of the group. All eyes were fixed on her. "A woman ejected from the family, who could certainly have the motive to want Marlene dead."

"What?" Teddy asked, his eyebrows narrowed in confusion.

Suddenly, one of the group stood and bolted. They ran past the chairs and out of the room, their footsteps thundering behind them on the stone floor.

Sandy turned to the officer and raised an eyebrow. "You'll want to catch them."

He turned and ran and the noise attracted the attention of the other police officers, three of whom returned from the banquet hall and ran after them.

Sandy met Tom's startled gaze and tried to hold her own tears back.

"She deserved it!" A voice screamed from the hallway, as the lead officer returned with the runaway in handcuffs. "You all deserved it! Now your family's broken just like mine!"

"Son?" Eli asked. He stood and walked across to the

doorway, where Hamm was restrained and surrounded by police. "What have you done?"

"I had no choice." Hamm muttered. "She ruined everything, dad."

"Oh Hamm." Eli said. He pushed past one officer and pulled his son in for a hug. "You stupid, stupid boy."

"You know mom cries for you every single night?" Hamm asked. "Every night I go into her room and ask if she's okay, and she tells me it's some book she's reading, but it's you. She cries for you, and for our family."

"You blamed your grandmother for your parents' breaking up." Sandy asked.

"Of course I do. And her inviting mom here and then humiliating her, it was the last straw. But, you're all as bad!" Hamm shouted to the group. "You all abandoned my mom. You were supposed to love her. You deserve each other."

"You've ruined everything, you fool!" Teddy shouted. "You've ruined this whole family."

"You just don't get it, do you?" Hamm said. "Your family ruined my family first."

"How on Earth could you think this was a good idea?" Eli asked.

"Because you and mom can be together now." Hamm said, and Sandy saw him again as the naive child she had caught a glimpse of earlier. "I sacrificed myself for you."

Eli collapsed to the ground and began to cry as the officers lead Hamm away.

"I love you, dad." He called.

15

*S*andy sat outside the B&B and watched as the sun rose over the sea, the pink shades dancing on the ocean waves. It was still cold, and she pulled her fleece jacket tighter around her body. She had given up on sleep in the early hours of the morning, when a nightmare had caused her to wake with tears streaming down her face.

Her bum was numb after hours of sitting on the cold, hard step. But her mind was clear.

Soon, she and Tom would begin the long drive back to Waterfell Tweed, less relaxed than she had hoped she would be after the trip.

"Penny for them?" Tom's voice asked. She turned to see him stood behind her in the porch.

"Hey." She said. "Good morning."

He closed the porch door and passed her a steaming hot mug of mocha, then sat next to her. "You doing ok?"

She nodded. "I can't stop thinking about Hamm."

"I can't stop thinking about Devon!" Tom said. "How did you figure out that she was trying to look guilty?"

"She didn't like that Hamm had sat next to Trixie at one

point. I thought that was odd. It made me wonder what she knew about him."

"What do you think will happen to him now?" Tom asked. "He's going to be a long way from his whole family."

"I think he wants it that way." Sandy said.

"It's all so sad."

Sandy nestled into his chest and gazed out to sea. "I'm glad you were with me, Tom. Without you, I'd have made this trip on my own and I…"

"You'd probably never have gone to Mull Castle, let's be honest." Tom said, with a grin. "I got you into this mess."

"Well, when you put it that way!" She teased. It felt odd to laugh after the high emotion of the day before.

"You were amazing yesterday." Tom said. He smelt of soap and opportunity. New beginnings.

"I wish I'd got to know Marlene McVeigh."

"She sounded like a force to be reckoned with." Tom said. "I think I'd have been a bit scared of her."

Sandy squeezed his arm and nestled closer to him. "I'm sorry our trip wasn't the relaxing break we hoped it would be."

He shrugged. "I wanted time with you. I got that."

She pulled away from him and raised an eyebrow up at him.

"Okay, it's not quite what I had in mind, but I'm learning that things are always a little unexpected with you, Sandy Shaw."

"Definitely unexpected." Sandy agreed. She caught sight of Tom's car parked across the road and remembered that their break was almost over. "What time do you want to hit the road?"

"The earlier the better really." He said with a sad smile.

"I'll go and pack." She said. She used Tom's leg to push

herself up to a standing position and heard a groan escape her. "Oh man, when did I start making those noises?"

"It comes to us all." Tom said. "I'd have thought carrying casks of ale would have kept me in shape but every time I pick one up I get winded."

"As if!" Sandy laughed. She couldn't believe Tom to be unfit in any way.

"It's true. Come and help out one day and we can compete, who can make the most groans!"

She shook her head and looked out to sea. "I really wish we weren't going home today."

The words surprised her. She loved Waterfell Tweed. She loved Books and Bakes. She missed her sister and, to her surprise, the black cat she had accidentally adopted. She was eager to get home, just maybe after an extra day or two with Tom.

"So, let's stay." Tom said.

"Very funny." Sandy said, then turned to see his expression. "You're serious, aren't you?"

"Absolutely. We can explain. Tanya would run the Tweed for a couple more days and I think Bernice can cope with Books and Bakes."

"Yeah, she can, but I'd feel bad asking her."

"You've got good people around you, Sand, they want to help you."

"Hmm." Sandy said. It was true that she didn't like asking for help. She'd told Bernice and Coral that she would be back at work the next day, and she didn't want to mess them around. "They're expecting me back."

Tom shrugged. "It's your choice. But I'd love to have some more time with you.

Sandy pursed her lips as she considered the choices. "I'll speak to Bernice."

She returned inside the B&B and took the stairs to her bedroom, where she sat on the bed and gazed out at the view. The lack of sleep was catching up with her. Her eyelids felt heavy and gravity seemed to pull her body into a lying position, but her mind was too active for sleep to find her.

Each time she blinked, she pictured Hamm's face. She hoped he would receive the help she felt he needed.

She picked up her phone and dialled the familiar number.

A breathless Bernice answered on the fourth ring. "Sandy? What's wrong?"

She let out a small laugh. "Nothing's wrong with me, or Tom. Things haven't been as relaxing as we'd hoped here, that's for sure. How are things at the shop?"

"Coral hasn't mastered the art of carrying two plates at once, if that's what you mean." Bernice said. It was good to hear her voice.

"Are you managing?"

"Of course I am." Bernice said, insulted by the question. "Look, if you're ringing to say you're staying longer with lover-boy, we'll be fine. You've got nothing to worry about."

Sandy let out a breath and laughed. "Am I that easy to read?"

"I know what's been happening." Bernice said. "Tom messaged me. Sounds like you need a couple of days to decompress."

"That's one word for it." Sandy admitted. "I can't believe Tom messaged you without telling me."

"He wanted to warn us, in case you did your normal and burst back into work as if nothing had happened. I'm glad you're being sensible. Enjoy your down time."

"I will, I promise. Thank you, Bernice."

"No need for thanks, Sand. It's my job."

"Bernice?" Sandy asked. "Will you explain to Coral and Cass? I think I'm going to turn my phone off for a couple of days, just really switch off from it all."

"Sounds perfect." Bernice said. "I'll let them know. Now, get off and enjoy yourself."

Sandy ended the call and caught her reflection in the bedroom mirror. Her face was mainly her smile.

She walked across to the window and pulled the old-fashioned fitting up so that the bottom half of the window opened. Her room was directly above the front door and she could see Tom's shape, still sat on the step where she had left him. He appeared to be gazing out to sea, his arms folded across his body for warmth.

"Tom!" She called. He spun around, taking a few moments to locate where her voice was coming from.

He looked at her hopefully.

"Fancy two more days?" She called, and watched as he punched the air in celebration.

"With you?" He asked. "Always."

THE END

THANK YOU FOR READING

If you're a lover of cozy mysteries, join my VIP Reader List.

Every Thursday, I send out an eMail packed with updates on my writing progress and life, plus special cozy mystery offers, free gifts, exclusive content and more.

Sign up now:

http://monamarple.com/wt4

ABOUT THE AUTHOR

Mona Marple is a mother, author and coffee enthusiast. She is creator of the Waterfell Tweed cozy mystery series and the Mystic Springs paranormal cozy mystery series.

You can see all of her books at author.to/MonaMarple

When she isn't busy writing a cozy mystery, she's probably curled up somewhere warm reading one.

She lives in England with her husband and daughter.

Connect with Mona:
www.MonaMarple.com
mona@monamarple.com

facebook.com/MonaMarpleAuthor

twitter.com/MonaMarple

instagram.com/MonaMarple

Printed in Great Britain
by Amazon

39604602R00071